SOME BRUISING MAY OCCUR

GARY McMAHON

JOURNALSTONE
YOUR LINK TO ARTIST TALENT

ISBN: 978-1-950305-22-3 (sc)
ISBN: 978-1-950305-23-0 (ebook)
Library of Congress Control Number: 2020934199

First printing edition: April 10, 2020
Published by JournalStone Publishing in the United States of America.
Cover Design and Layout: Don Noble/Rooster Republic Press
Interior Layout: Yara Eloff & Scarlett R. Algee
Edited by Sean Leonard
Proofread by Scarlett R. Algee

JournalStone Publishing
3205 Sassafras Trail
Carbondale, Illinois 62901

JournalStone books may be ordered through booksellers or by contacting:
JournalStone | www.journalstone.com

TABLE OF CONTENTS

ACKNOWLEDGMENTS

This book is dedicated to my wife and son. I love you both more than I can say.

Thanks to the editors who published some of these stories and all the writer friends who have helped me along the way. We currently live in terrible, troubled times, with a lot of us stuck in lockdown due to the global Covid-19 pandemic, and we are being reminded in a very real way that nobody can accomplish anything worthwhile without the help of others.

I'm not at all sure that more horror stories are what the world really needs right now, but I humbly offer these tales as a distraction from the real horrors—I'm afraid they're all I have. Be safe, be kind, be good to each other.

"These dark things
I give to thee
Shadow-soft fruit
From a midnight tree"

-Anon

SOME
BRUISING
MAY OCCUR

INTRODUCTION

BY ALISON LITTLEWOOD

WHAT CAN I SAY ABOUT Gary McMahon? He's one of the first people I met in the genre, and it's always a pleasure. We've laughed over a pint at Fantasycon and enjoyed a curry and generally put the world to rights, as well as sharing space in several anthologies. I've read his work in *Black Static* and many other fine publications, and enjoyed the *Concrete Grove* trilogy and *Pretty Little Dead Things* and admired his gritty vision of what can be achieved in contemporary horror fiction. So it's a great honour to drop by and introduce this, Gary's latest collection of short stories.

And very fine stories they are. It includes some of my favourites: 'My Boy Builds Coffins,' 'Unicorn Meat,' 'The Hanging Boy,' and 'The Night Just Got Darker,' the author's touching tribute to the late Joel Lane. It tells of a man who writes in order to make the bleak world bearable, 'working and reworking just to hold back the darkness'.

And that feels entirely fitting within the world of Gary McMahon. These are not stories about sunshine and flowers; they are most definitely from the author of *The Concrete Grove*. They are urban, modern, unflinching tales of inner cities and back streets, of waste lands and decaying things. Outside the door are not trees and fields, but rundown housing estates and boarded-up factories and asbestos garages; litter and abandoned furniture and the loss of hope. The settings are ones we can all recognise, so that when the author deftly introduces a savour of the unsettling and the unknown, our sense of unease is deeper for the contrast.

Similarly, here are not monsters, but the people we know—or think we do, so that when the unexpected intrudes, it is all the more disturbing. ('He looked entirely normal; he was the same as always, her beautiful little boy. He wasn't a monster. He hadn't been taken over by some alien force. He was her boy. He built coffins.')

McMahon's characters are fully rounded. These are people we feel to have lived, who are bruised by life, whose insights are the result of suffering. ('I just think that maybe...maybe you have to be damaged in a certain way to be able to see it.') Some are brutal and brutalised, who don't quite feel they belong in the lives in which they've found themselves; they don't fit in their own skin. They are battered people, hurt people; they are damaged in a certain way.

As good horror can, these stories imbue the ordinary with a sense of the mythic and the symbolic; they have resonance. Everyday things become terrifying. A door. A wall. A father or a son. Suddenly what is safe isn't safe any longer, not in the hands of Gary McMahon. He tears away any veils of comfort, leaving only stark reality behind; telling us the truth.

These stories are chilling, yes, but even as you read, they also demand something from you, even if only a pause, a deep breath, time to reflect. They reach deep inside you and grab what they can with their claws. They pass from the messy, frightening world of children to the messy, frightening and equally unknowable world of adulthood, and show us the terrors in each.

And yet there is beauty here too. There is love and kindness and an appreciation of the ineffable mysteries of the world, something other than the bleakness we have made, even if glimpsed only in the midst of its loss. These stories give us a sense of the things we should value and grasp and try to hold onto. Even when mired in the sordid, there is something beyond it: 'He was rubbing her thigh, his broad fingers gripping her slightly too tightly. The bruises there began to sing. She could hear them, like a chorus of castrati: high, beautiful, the voices of weeping angels.'

To sum up, I will simply say that here is a writer at the height of his skills. I'm happy to know him, and to have had the pleasure of reading much of his fiction. I have always found it excellent, well-deserving of the reputation Gary has built for himself, and I'm glad to report that this collection is no exception.

And so—welcome to the world of Gary McMahon. These stories are constructed simply of words, but beware, for they can nevertheless plunge a knife into your gut. They have power. They will take you by the hand and lead you to places you don't expect, and when you return, you might just be a little bit changed. This is writing that blisters and burns and scars—and so, Dear Reader, I must warn you: some bruising may occur...

Alison Littlewood

MY BOY BUILDS COFFINS

SUSAN FOUND THE FIRST ONE when she was tidying his room.

Chris was at school, and she'd been sprucing up the house before popping off to collect him after the afternoon session. The ground floor was done; the lounge was spick and span (as her mother had loved to say) and the kitchen was so clean it belonged in a show home. The downstairs bathroom was clean enough for a royal inspection. The en-suite would do, she supposed, and her and Dan's bedroom was the best it could be, considering they both liked to dump their dirty clothes all over the floor and the furniture.

Now it was time to tackle Chris's room, which was about as messy as any eight-year-old could hope to achieve.

She pushed open the door, holding her breath, and walked into the chaos. His blow-up punch bag had been moved into the centre of the room and left there. The floor was littered with books, magazines, Top Trumps playing cards, rogue counters from board games, art supplies, and—oddly—old cardboard toilet roll holders.

"Jesus, Chris..." She tiptoed across the room to the window, trying not to step on anything that might break. When she got there, she pushed open the window to let in some fresh air. The room smelled stale, as if it hadn't been lived in for months.

"Okay," she murmured. "Let's get this shit sorted."

First she tackled the floor. Patiently, she picked up everything and put it away where it belonged—or at least where she thought it belonged, or where it looked like it belonged. After twenty minutes the room was already looking much better. At least she could move around without fear of treading on something.

Next she tidied up the top of his desk—where she found old DVDs without cases, more playing cards, flakes of dried modelling clay, small stones from the garden, bits and pieces of magic tricks, and other sundry boy-items.

The desk was almost clear, and she was looking for a drawer into which she could squeeze yet more art supplies, when she found the coffin.

It was in the bottom drawer, where at one time Chris had kept his football shirts—one a year, from birth, because his dad supported Manchester United.

She stood silently and stared into the drawer. It was empty but for the coffin.

It was made out of what looked to be a fine-grade timber—pale, with a neat wood-grained pattern. The wood was unpainted and untreated; it was bare, nude, but smooth, as if it had been sanded. Attached to the lid of the coffin was a small brass plate with the word "Daddy" engraved across it in a neat, delicate script.

For a moment Susan felt as if someone else had entered the room behind her. She resisted the urge to turn and look, but she felt a presence there. She knew it was nonsense, there was no one there, but all the same she sensed it. Standing right behind her, perhaps even peering over her shoulder. At the coffin.

She moved to her knees and looked closer. The coffin was small. It was probably the right size to hold an Action Man doll ("It isn't a doll," Chris always protested, "it's an action figure!") and she wondered if that was indeed what the casket contained.

Carefully, she reached into the drawer and placed her hands on the sides of the coffin. She lifted it out of the drawer, stood, and carried it over to the bed. She put it down and thought about what she was going to do.

Then, on impulse that wasn't really an impulse because she'd been planning it all along, she reached down and lifted the lid off the coffin.

Inside was a thin layer of dirt. She ran her fingers through the dirt, feeling its gritty reality. It felt soft and slightly damp, like soil from the garden.

"What the hell is this?"

Part of her tensed in anticipation of a reply from that unseen figure: the one that wasn't there, oh no, not really there at all. Because she was all alone in her son's room, wasn't she?

II

She broached the subject over dinner that evening.

Chris was tucking into his chicken, gravy smeared across his lips and his cheeks: the boy couldn't eat anything without wearing it. Dan was reading a computer printout at the table as he nibbled at his own meal, taking small, delicate bites. She was so sick of asking him not to read at the table that she'd stopped saying it over a month ago.

"Chris."

The boy looked up from his meal. He smiled. "Yes, Mummy?" His teeth were covered in gravy, too.

"I tidied your room today."

"Sorry, Mummy. I meant to do it, but I forgot."

She sighed. "Yes, I know...just like you forget everything, except sweets and comics and DVDs."

He grinned. "Can I watch a DVD tonight?"

"No," said Dan, putting down his printout. "It's a school night. That's a weekend treat."

Chris began to pout. He picked at his chicken with his fork. The tines scraped against the plate, making Susan wince. He'd stopped having the tantrums over a month ago, but there was always the risk that he'd go off on one again.

"Listen, Chris...about your room."

"Yeah." He didn't look up—he was sulking.

"I found something. In a drawer."

Dan glanced at her, raising his eyebrows in a question. She shook her head: she would deal with this.

"Mummy found something...a little bit strange."

Chris looked up from his food. He was frowning. "What was it?"

"Let me show you." She stood and pushed her chair away from the table. She crossed the room and took the coffin out of the cupboard, where she'd put it for safekeeping. She carried it back to the table, cleared the condiments out of the way, and set it down in front of her family. It felt ritualistic, like the beginning of some obscure rite. She pushed the thought away. It wasn't helpful.

"This is what I found."

Dan stared at the coffin. His face wasn't sure what expression to form. Chris smiled at her.

"Do you know what this is, Chris?"

Dan glanced at his son, remaining silent for now.

"Yes. It's a box." The boy reached out for the coffin, but she moved it across the table and out of his way, as if it might infect him or something.

"Where did you get it, darling?" She was trying to keep things light, but a strange mood had begun to descend upon the dining table. It felt as if a shadow had entered the room, dimming the lights, and the temperature had dropped by a few degrees. "Well, Chris? Where did you get this...box? Where did it come from?"

"I made it, Mummy. I made it for Daddy." He turned to face Dan, his small face beaming, his eyes large and expectant, as if he'd done something miraculous and was due a large reward. Some sweets, perhaps. Or a new DVD.

"I..." Dan looked from her to the boy, and then back again. "Thank you," he said, absurdly. Then he looked at Susan again, searching for help. "Did you make it at school?"

"No. Here. At home." Chris's smile dropped. His small face seemed to crumple inwards. He was clearly making a concerted effort not to lose his temper, despite the odd situation, and Susan loved him for it.

"Well, who taught you how to make it? I mean, *someone* must have helped you."

The boy shook his head, refusing to say anything more.

"Well?"

He shook his head again.

Susan intervened before things became more fractious: "Okay, you pop off and get your jim-jams on, and after you've done your teeth, I'll read to you for a while before you go to sleep."

Dan walked away, obviously troubled. Chris dragged his feet as he slowly left the room.

III

"So what the hell's going on here?" Dan was pacing the floor and drinking whisky. He looked harried. His hair was a mess from where he'd been running his fingers through it—like he always did when he was stressed. His face was pale and his shirt was hanging out of the waistband of his trousers. "I mean, this isn't...normal. It isn't normal behaviour, is it?"

"Just calm down a minute. Let's think this through."

"That's easy for you to say," he said, his shoulders slumping. "He didn't build *you* a coffin."

"He's eight years old, Dan. He doesn't know what he's doing. He probably saw it in a magazine or something. Or on the telly. I bet he thought he was doing something nice for you."

Dan laughed: a single barking sound. "Fucking hell, Susan." He only ever called her that when he was anxious; usually it was *Sue*. "Maybe we should call someone. A doctor...or a psychiatrist. Get him seen to again. Maybe this is to do with the old trouble."

"Don't be silly. You're overreacting. We don't need anyone. He's over all that anger business. This is...different. Something we can cope with ourselves."

Dan did not seem convinced. "You saw the craftsmanship on that thing. Look at it." He strode across the room and picked up the coffin. His mouth twisted into an unconscious grimace, as if he were touching something rotten. "Look at it. The perfectly mitred joints, the smooth finish...this is *beautiful* work." The way he said that word, he gave it the opposite effect to what it really meant. "An eight-year-old kid can't do this kind of work..." He sat down in the armchair, looking tired and defeated. He still held the coffin, but loosely. He didn't seem to want to let it go.

"I don't pretend to understand this either, honey, but I think we need to tread carefully...just in case it triggers an episode or something."

He was rubbing the side of the coffin with his thumb. "It's got dirt inside...grave dirt."

"Don't be silly."

"*Grave* dirt," he said again, as if repetition might diminish the power of the words. "My grave..."

"It's soil from the garden." She got up and walked over to him, snatched away the coffin. She moved over to the fireplace and put the coffin down on the mantelpiece, next to last year's school photo: Chris smiled at her from inside the frame, his hair neatly combed, his shirt collars sticking out from the neck of his grey school sweater, his cheeks shining from the heat of the photographer's lights. He looked like a typical small boy, but underneath it all he'd been a mess of conflicting emotions, a child governed by an inexplicable rage.

"Okay," said Dan, behind her. "So we tread softly." He sounded more relaxed, less wound up.

She turned around. He was still seated, and pouring another large shot of whisky into the glass. "Could I have one of those?" She held out her own glass, but made no move to approach him. "I could really use it." She smiled.

He nodded.

She walked over, but instead of waiting for him to pour, she knelt down before him and ran her hands across his thighs. "It'll be okay. He's just a kid. He had no idea of the effect something like this might have."

"But the workmanship..." Dan's face was pleading. It made him look years younger, almost like a child himself.

"I know...it's weird, I'll admit that. But that's all it is—weird and unusual. There's nothing to worry about. I promise. We'll deal with it, as a family. No more pills and doctors."

IV

A few days later she found the second coffin.

This one had been left on her bed. It was a Saturday and Dan was out playing five-a-side football, making cross-field runs and dirty tackles just to relax. She was hanging up some clothes, and when she turned around from the wardrobe to face the room, the coffin was there, on her pillow. The brass plate on this one read "Mummy."

It hadn't been there when she entered the room. She was sure. She would have noticed.

"Chris?"

There was no reply. The house was quiet. Outside, she could hear traffic on the nearby main road, some kids shouting on another street, and the sound of someone mowing their lawn. They were real noises, the sounds that connected you to reality. There was nothing to fear here, in this friendly little neighbourhood.

"Are you there, baby?"

She heard a shuffling sound in the hall. For a moment, she was afraid to cross the room and look through the doorway. Some unreasonable fear held her there, afraid of her own home. Her own son. The noises outside now seemed as if they were miles away, part of some other, safer world.

She recalled the worst of his rages, not that long ago. He'd left her battered and bruised, but the worst pain was in knowing that someone created from her own flesh and blood was capable of losing control to such a startling degree.

But that was over now. He was better. They'd worked things out, with the help of a good child psychologist and some medication. There was no need to go back, to return to any of that. This time was different.

"Chris!" She used the strength of her resolve to fuel her and moved quickly to the door. When she looked outside, the landing was empty. Sunlight lanced through the landing window, capturing the dust motes in the air like flecks of epidermis suspended in fluid. She went back inside the room and sat down on the bed.

She stared at the coffin on the pillow.

Outside, the sound of the lawn mower cut out. The screaming kids moved away and their din began to fade. The traffic noises seemed to quieten.

Susan reached out and lifted up the lid of the coffin. As she'd expected, inside was a thin layer of soil. She picked up the coffin and shook it, disturbing the loose particles of earth. As she watched, something was uncovered. She reached inside with her forefinger and thumb, pushing aside the soil, and picked out an object. It was her wedding ring. She looked at her hand—at her wedding finger—and saw a pale band of flesh, a tan line where the ring should have been.

This was new. There had been nothing but dirt in Dan's coffin.

Her stomach tightened; her head began to throb dully. She couldn't remember taking off her wedding ring. In fact, she hardly ever did so, not even in the bath or the shower. She was superstitious; she liked to keep it on, so as not to tempt fate. She remembered an old friend who'd lost her wedding ring, and three months later her husband had dropped dead from a sudden heart attack. Nonsense, she realised, but still...you just never could tell.

Things like this were symbolic. Things like wedding rings. And coffins.

She glanced up, looking at the doorway. There was no sound. No movement. Just dead air, empty space.

Susan put the lid back on the coffin and backed away from the bed, as if it were some kind of ferocious animal that had come into the room. She picked up her mobile phone from the bedside table, and then she wondered who the hell she was thinking of calling anyway. Dan? Her mother? The fucking police?

This was stupid. It was insane.

Her boy built coffins—that was all. There was nothing wrong with that, not really. It was just a bit strange, a little offbeat. No harm done;

nobody was getting hurt. At least he was taking an interest in arts and crafts.

Susan stifled a mad giggle.

She put down the phone and left the room, leaving the coffin in there.

Chris's room was just along the hall. She could see from where she was standing that his door was shut. She walked along the landing and stood outside, listening. She couldn't hear a thing from inside his room, not even his television or his music playing.

She reached out and grabbed the door handle, turned it, pushed open the door.

Chris was sitting on his bed reading a book. He glanced up as she stepped inside. He smiled. He looked entirely normal; he was the same as always, her beautiful little boy. He wasn't a monster. He hadn't been taken over by some alien force. He was her boy. He built coffins.

"Everything okay, son?"

He nodded. "I'm reading." He held up his book, cover facing outwards, for her to see. "Moshi Monsters," he said. "I love them." He turned his attention back to the book; his face became serious as he continued to read.

"Chris?"

"Yeah." He was distracted. He didn't want to talk. He wanted to read. He'd always loved books, even when he was being a brat. He was a good little reader—top of the class in English. Maths, too. A clever boy. A good kid. A reader. A builder of coffins.

"Did you put something in Mummy's room earlier? When I was hanging up the clothes. Did you bring me a present?"

"Yes." He nodded. "I built you a box. Just like Daddy's."

She swallowed. Her throat was dry. "Why, baby? Why did you build Mummy a box?" It was the first time the question had been asked. She and Dan had agreed to approach the situation with caution, in case they said the wrong thing or pushed too hard. They'd been monitoring Chris—his moods, his speech, everything they could think of. He'd been just the same as always...their bright young son, mended now. Nothing was different. He was acting the same as always.

Apart from this, she thought. *Apart from the coffins*. And the thought made her admit that they were lying to each other. Chris *was* acting different, and they were both too confused and afraid to confront these changes in their boy. His rages might be over, but something else had replaced them. These days he was...secretive. He kept things from them. Things like this: the origins of his coffin-making.

"I thought you'd like one." Still, he didn't look up from his book.

"Why's that, baby?" She took another step inside the room, letting the door shut behind her.

"Dunno. Just thought you would." He looked up, smiling.

"Where did you get the soil, baby? The soil you put in the...boxes."

"Out of the hole."

The world seemed to compress around her, threatening to crush her. "What hole?"

"The one outside, in the garden. The magic hole, down beside the back wall."

As if in a dream, she moved across the room and stood at the window. She looked down at the garden to the rear of the house, taking in the expansive lawn, the trees that grew alongside the dividing fence, and the small water feature Dan had put in three summers ago. There was a dry stone wall at the bottom boundary, separating their garden from the field beyond. The grass and bushes there were overgrown; Dan had neglected the area because he said he liked it to look wild, like the countryside.

Wild. Untamed.

"Where's this hole, baby? Tell Mummy where the magic hole is."

He was still on the bed. Still reading. He seemed utterly unconcerned. "Down there...at the bottom of the garden. Right next to where we buried Mr. Jump last year."

Mr. Jump was Chris's pet rabbit. He'd frozen to death the previous winter, and they'd conducted a small family funeral involving an old shoe box, a children's Bible, and two flimsy wooden lolly sticks glued together in a cruciform pattern to make a grave marker.

"Okay, baby. Thank you. Thanks for making me the box."

She turned away and left the room, walking back along the landing and down the stairs. She counted the stairs as she descended, just to help herself remain calm. She wasn't sure what she was supposed to be frightened of, but she was terrified. It was like being a child again, fearful of the dark but not knowing why; scared of the unknown.

She sat down in the kitchen and waited for the kettle to boil; then she made a pot of tea and waited for Dan to come home, rubbing at her bare wedding finger with the ball of her thumb.

V

They waited until Chris was asleep. They didn't want to disturb him, and if he saw them digging around out there he might start to feed off their fear. They were sure of nothing, but they knew that they didn't want to give their son any cause for further confusion.

It crossed Susan's mind that this was what they did in every horror film she'd ever seen: they waited for darkness before making their move. It always ended badly.

"What the hell do you think we're going to find out there?" Dan was standing by the back door, bathed in the light from the kitchen. He was holding a shovel and wearing his gardening clothes—torn jeans, a baggy sweater, and thick leather gloves. Susan held the torch.

"I have no idea, but we have to take a look. Don't we?" She

realised that she wanted him to say no. She was desperate for him to put the brakes on the situation and make them both return indoors. She didn't want to make the decisions; she wanted him to step up and take control.

"I suppose you're right."

She waited for a moment, looking up at the sky, searching for inspiration. It was black, the stars were tiny, and the moon was nothing but a pale, undistinguished saucer amid the wispy clouds. "I'm scared," she said.

Dan took a few steps towards her, paused, and then came the rest of the way. He rested the shovel against the wall and put his arms around her, drawing her close. "I know...but this is our son we're talking about. We have to find out what's going on. What choice do we have?"

She nodded against his shoulder, saying nothing. This wasn't a horror film; it was real life. Even if things got messy, she and Dan would sort it all out. It's what people did, in real life.

"Who the hell are we meant to turn to for help? We don't even know what's going on." Her voice was strained.

Dan pressed against her. "We'll think about that when we have some facts."

She nodded again, closed her eyes and sniffed at him. She'd always loved how he smelled; his aroma was a comfort. Whenever he was away on business, she slept with his football shirt on her pillow, just so she could smell him in the night.

"Let's go," she whispered.

He pulled away and grabbed the shovel. She followed him across the grass, along the fence line, to the bottom of the garden, pointing the jittery torch beam ahead of them. They kicked at the weeds, looking for anything that might be called a hole. At first they didn't see a thing, but after a short while Susan stumbled, almost twisting her ankle as she stepped on the edge of the hole.

"Here," she whispered. "I've found it." She reached down and rubbed at her ankle.

"Why are you whispering?

"I have no fucking idea." It was a funny moment, she supposed, but neither of them laughed.

Dan started pulling at the weeds, tearing them out and throwing them against the dry stone wall. She put down the torch and bent down to help him, peering into the hole. It was small—about the same diameter as her soup pan at home—but it looked deep. It was too dark to tell exactly how deep, but she couldn't see the bottom, even when she shone the torch's beam directly into the hole.

Before long they'd cleared away the weeds and the overgrown grass from around the hole. It was remarkably neat and round, as if it had been bored into the ground by a machine. Susan knelt down at the side of the hole and bent over it, trying again to judge its depth.

"Here," said Dan. "Drop this down." He handed her a small, smooth stone.

She dropped the stone down the hole. Waited. Didn't hear it hit bottom. Picking up the torch again, she shone the light down the hole, but it was swallowed by the darkness down there.

"What the fuck?" said Dan.

She turned and looked at him. He was nothing but a dark silhouette standing against the sky; he had no face. He was form without substance.

"Let's just cover it over," she said. "Fill it in and forget about it."

"No," said Dan. "I have to know."

"Have to know what?"

He leaned down towards her. For once, she failed to detect his comforting smell. "I don't know."

Dan started digging. She moved out of the way, staying well back to give him some room. He dug the hole wider, creating a circular pit roughly two feet in diameter. The pit tapered inwards, down towards the original hole, which sat at its centre, black and threatening.

"You can't just keep digging," she said. "What if you never reach the end?"

Dan paused in his labour, wiping the sweat from his brow with the back of his hand. "What else can I do?"

He resumed digging, hunched over the shovel like an old man.

Susan glanced up at Chris's bedroom window. The curtains were closed and the lights were off, but she was certain that she could make out the shape of someone standing there, perhaps watching them. She closed her eyes, wishing it away, but when she opened them again the shape was still there. She stared at it for a long time, and eventually it blended into the background, becoming less clear, a stain on the fabric of night. Perhaps there had been nothing there all along.

"Shit," said Dan.

She looked over at him. He stopped digging and glanced up at her, looking into her eyes.

Slowly, Dan bent down and moved something around with his fingers in the ditch. He straightened up, holding whatever it was in his hands. He leaned forward, into the light, and held out his hands to show her what he'd found.

Dan was holding what Susan supposed must be some of Mr. Jump's bones. But there was something wrong with them: they were twisted, distorted, as if proximity to the hole had warped them, pulled them out of shape. The skull was elongated, weasel-like; the ribs were fused together, like white armour, and the forelegs were crooked, ending in grasping, claw-like bony paws.

Dan threw away the bones, scattering them into the darkness. A look of intense distaste crossed his face, and then he picked up the shovel and continued with his task.

It wasn't long before the shovel scraped against something solid.

"What is it?"

"I think...I think it's a coffin."

"Another one?"

He shook his head. "This one's bigger."

Susan stood and helped him clear away the earth from the coffin. It looked exactly the same as the others, except it was much larger. It was made from the same fine timber, possessed a similar hand-rubbed finish, and had a brass plate attached to the lid. When Susan shone the torch onto the coffin lid, the word she saw etched onto the plate made her go cold.

It said "Son."

By the time they'd unearthed the coffin in its entirety, the sun was starting to rise. The sky in the east was smeared with red; the clouds there looked painted on. It took both of them to manhandle the coffin out of the hole, but still it wasn't too heavy.

"Shall we..."

"Open it?"

Susan nodded. She knew there would be nothing in there, except perhaps some more dirt. It wasn't heavy enough to have anything more substantial inside. But they had to be sure. They could leave nothing to chance.

Dan used the shovel to wedge open the lid. He slid the sharp end of the shovel's blade into the joint and stepped on the handle. The lid popped open with the sound of splintering wood; it jerked to one side, revealing a glimpse of the interior. Dan bent down and heaved the lid across the coffin, shoving it onto the ground at the side of the hole. The coffin was filled almost to the top with torn scraps of paper, like the cheap packaging that came with items sent through the post.

"I don't want to see." Susan took a step backwards, away from the coffin.

Dan ignored her. He reached down and began to push the paper out of the way, scattering some of the scraps across the ground.

Susan held her breath. She saw a flash of colour: pale pink, like the petals of the roses in her garden. It was skin. Human skin. Dan kept clearing away the paper, and she knew what she was going to see even before it was uncovered. She tried to deny the sight, but she couldn't. She wished herself blind, but it didn't work.

Son.

Lying in repose, with his hands crossed neatly over his chest, was Chris. He was naked. His shallow chest had sunken slightly; his forearms were unbearably thin. His face was narrow, like that of an old man. He looked like he'd been dead for a long time, but not long enough for his body to rot. It was as if something were keeping him that way, cold and lifeless, yet pristine: like the sanctified remains of a saint.

"Dan... Oh, Dan. What the hell is it?"

Dan fell down onto his knees and lifted the corpse partially out of the coffin. The body was obviously light; Dan lifted it with ease and stumbled slightly. The arms slid away from the chest, the head tilted to one side, the dark hair falling wispily across the thin white face; the bony legs bent and the knees came up, as if it were trying to stand.

"No," said Dan, as if he couldn't quite accept what he was seeing, what he was holding. "Oh, no...fuck no. Not this."

Susan looked up at Chris's bedroom window. The figure was still there, but now the curtains were open. The figure was small—much smaller and thinner than their son. The figure's hands looked unnaturally long, and seemed to wriggle too many fingers as they reached up to twitch the curtains further apart. As it flapped limply forward, pressing its dark, smooth face up against the glass, she was reminded of a crudely fashioned doll or a puppet—something animated, but clumsily; a thing that should never have been given life, a hastily assembled imitation of the human form.

She turned back to her husband and sank to the ground. He was sitting on the ground, rocking and wailing as he clasped their pale son to his breast. "He's too light...there's nothing left inside him..."

Dan looked up and turned their boy's face towards her. It was oddly blank, as if waiting for an expression to be carved there. His body looked light, empty, just as much of a puppet as the thing now capering inside his room. "...nothing left inside..."

Dazed, afraid, confused to the point of idiocy, Susan rose slowly and awkwardly to her feet and started walking stiffly towards the house. Whatever was in there—whatever had taken the essence of her son, her wonderful son who'd built such fine, fine coffins—she would find it and she would kill it. Before she lost her sanity completely, she would make it pay.

Susan dropped the torch. She would not need light where she was going. It might, in fact, be better to work in darkness.

As she became more sure-footed and began to run, she made herself a promise: Before this day was done, she would force whatever had replaced Chris into a tiny coffin of its own, and dance upon its grave.

SOME PICTURES IN AN ALBUM

THE BOOK IS A SLIM *faux leather photograph album.*

The front cover is dusty and stained, and scratched crudely into the material is a circular design that matches the birthmark behind my right knee.

The very edges of the plastic pages are crumpled and torn. It's an ordinary album, something that might be stored in the loft spaces of a million family homes around the country.

Nothing strange. Nothing unusual.

Now that my father is dead, it's just another item found among his belongings...but for some reason I'm drawn to this particular album as I sort through his stuff to box it all up and send it to the charity shop.

I sit down on the bed in my old room and open the book.

Each of the seventeen photographs has its own page; every white-bordered Polaroid image is positioned perfectly at the centre and covered in a thin plastic protective flap. Someone has taken a lot of time to put the album together. A lot of love went into the preparation.

I always called him my father, not Dad. He was never that...he was always just a father. I can't imagine why he would take so much care in the preparation of this album, or why he would have wanted to keep the pictures I find inside.

- The first photograph shows me standing in front of a high red-brick wall. I am six years old. I recognise myself, but it's like looking into a mirror at a reflection that isn't quite right.

I'm holding above my head a small silver plastic replica of the F.A. cup with red and white ribbons tied around it. There is a long, thin shadow on the wall beside me. It is 1973, the year Sunderland beat Leeds in the Cup Final to produce a now legendary example of "giant killing." My face is joyous; my rosy cheeks are soft; my reddish hair almost matches the colour of the bricks behind me. I am wearing a light blue shirt that looks like it has lighter blue flowers on it. My entire chest is hidden by a red and white rosette and a knitted red and white doll, both pinned to the shirt.

• The next photograph, on the adjoining page, shows simply a black door. It looks like the front door to a normal terraced house. The bricks around it are of the same shade of red as those in the previous photo, but they are more weathered. The edge of a window frame can be seen on the right of the shot. The door itself looks old, beaten. Paint is flaking off to expose patches of the cheap pale timber beneath.

• Over the page is a photograph of me on one of those mechanical animal rides that used to be outside shops on the high street in most English towns. Put in a couple of coins and let your kid ride for a few minutes. This one is a cartoon elephant. I am clutching its ears. My smile is huge. I am wearing a blue woollen hat. My mother—looking so young, so pretty— is standing to the side, smiling shyly. The arm and leg of what I assume to be my father can be seen next to her, the rest of him just clipped out of the frame. My body is slightly blurred because of the motion of the ride, but my face is perfectly still. I seem to be glimpsing something incredible. There is a light in my eyes that is difficult to define. A question occurs to me as I stare at the image: If my parents are both in the shot, who is that taking the photograph?

• Next up is the outside of a shop: a corner newsagent, Moses & Sons. Faded posters stuck up with tape in the window; a man in a white overcoat can be glimpsed behind the glass, standing at a counter. The window display is mostly sweets, with a few piles of comics and magazines. I am standing with my back to the camera, looking through the window. My face is reflected in the glass; I am not smiling. At first glance it appears that I might be crying, but it isn't clear. Perhaps I am simply concentrating on all the sugared treats in the display. There is another figure reflected in the glass window beside me, this one tall and thin, but whoever it is cannot be seen in the frame.

• The door again—at least it looks like the same one. A little older, maybe. More worn. This photograph is darker than the last one, so it could have been taken at a different time of day. Later. Closer to dark. I begin to suspect that each photograph represents a new time frame. Perhaps a year has passed since the last one.

• Over the page there are two blank sheets. No photos here, just the empty clear plastic flaps. It's as if a year has been missed, or deliberately excised.

• Me, nine years old. I know this because I can recall the scene clearly. My birthday. In the photograph I am surrounded by crumpled balls of wrapping paper and presents. A cowboy rifle, an Action Man tank, several cars and an assortment of books. My father's foot can be seen at the bottom left corner of the frame. He is wearing the worn brown slippers I always remember, the pair with the hard rubber soles. The ones he used to like beating me with. He never wanted to hurt me, or so he said at the time. He always gave me a choice: the slipper or an hour spent locked up in the cubby hole under the stairs. I always chose the slipper, because it was over quickly and I didn't like the dark under the stairs—or the thought of what it might contain.

• The door again. This year it is cleaner, as if someone has given it a lick of paint. The handle has been replaced. The letter box shines. Sunlight is reflected off the golden knocker, making bright patterns on the camera lens.

• The next photograph is disturbing. It shows me sitting on the lap of a man I do not recognise. His eyes are large and empty; his creamy white hands are massive as they drape over my shoulders, and at least some of the fingers are resting at a weird angle, as if they are in fact boneless. I look...well, my expression is unreadable. I am staring directly into the camera, but not smiling. There could be an element of pleading in my eyes, but that might just be the current me reading too much into a blank expression. My mother, dressed in flared pants and an ugly tie-dye blouse, stands to the side, leaning in the doorway that leads into the kitchen. She seems worried; her eyes are dull and she is biting her bottom lip. Her shoulders are slumped. I cannot remember ever seeing her look so deflated;

she was always such a happy woman. The man whose lap I occupy doesn't look quite right. His hair is odd. His face is a different colour to his elongated hands. Is he wearing a wig? Is that a mask?

- The door. Soiled. Burn marks across the kickboard. The knocker has been removed. The letterbox is stuffed with dead leaves.

- In the next one, I'm ten. I'm sitting on a red Raleigh Chopper bike in the street, my legs too short to allow my feet to properly touch the ground. I'm balanced on my tiptoes, the bike leaning slightly to the right and towards a low garden wall. It must be cold, because I'm wrapped up warm: a thick coat, a matching Sunderland AFC hat and scarf, woollen fingerless gloves on my hands. My smile is awkward, as if it is forced. Again, I have no recollection of this photo being taken, but I do remember the day my father brought the bike home after work—it was stolen later that same day, taken from outside our house when I left it leaning against the wall to pop inside for dinner. I got the slipper for that, too. My father carried on longer than usual, and he was crying when he finished. I have the uneasy feeling that there was someone else there, in the room, when my punishment was meted out: an unseen audience, watching silently from a corner of the back bedroom. Afterwards, I couldn't sit down for hours because of the pain in my buttocks. I remember that part most of all.

- The door. Hinges rusted. Wood blackened. This time it's ajar. I can see the gap, only blackness visible. I wish I could remember this door, where it was, what it led to. It certainly wasn't the door to our house: that was green, and had a lot of glass panels. The door to a family home. This door is different; less welcoming. Nobody would willingly knock on this door or want to see who lives behind it.

• Eleven years old, in the back yard. I'm turned away from the camera, pinning young Shelley Cork to the wall with one arm on either side of her pretty face, the palms of my hands pressed hard against the bricks. We're kissing. My eyes are closed; hers are open. She looks panicked, but she doesn't seem to be struggling. I do have a memory of this, but it's much different. We were necking against the wall at the back of our house, practicing kissing like grown-ups, testing boundaries. She rested her hand against my crotch; I stuck my hand down the back of her knickers and groped her arse. There was nobody else there, so I don't know how this photograph exists. It should not be here. In my memory, Shelley wasn't panicked at all. She was excited, exhilarated. Her breathing was heavy against the side of my face; her eyes kept blinking and she pulled me tightly against her warm, soft body. The whole thing was her idea; I was the one who was afraid. I didn't want my father to come out and catch us in the act. I remember feeling a similar kind of unreasonable guilt later that same year, when Shelley Cork went missing.

• Again, we have the black door. It's half open, and this time a thin, pale hand can be seen gripping its edge. The fingers are too long, and there are only three of them, but with too many joints. The knuckle bones jut out unnaturally. The skin is a sickly yellowy shade of cream.

• I'm twelve years old, sitting down by the river with my legs dangling over the rocks, the soles of my running shoes hanging mere inches above the water. Along the riverbank, on the opposite side, people are fishing. I'm not watching them. I'm staring down into the black water. My posture is strange, strained, as if I'm poised to jump. I used to go down there a lot, but this photograph seems alien, as if it isn't me there by the river, but someone else imitating me. A freakishly tall figure in the bushes directly opposite me, on the other side of the water, stands and stares.

• This time the door is wide open. The wood is rotten and splintered; the door hangs askew in its frame, the hinges damaged. Beyond the angled wooden rectangle, there is visible the rear view of someone walking along a scruffy hallway and into the interior of the house. The wallpaper is hanging in strips, the bare boards are warped and stained, and the figure is fading into the dark at the end of the hallway. The figure is naked. Its skin is the colour of curdled cream. The bones of its spine stick out like a line of pebbles. The figure is tall and terribly thin, like a prisoner in one of those concentration camp photographs from WWII. Its legs are bent in the wrong place; its arms are so long that its three-fingered hands almost touch the floor. Its head—or what little of it can be seen—is smooth and almost hairless, like that of a baby.

• The next photograph is a close-up portrait shot. My face is framed nicely, centred on the page. The background is blurred, out of focus, so it could be anywhere. I am screaming. My eyes are so wide that at first I don't recognise my own face, and my mouth is stretched open to the limit. My face is pale but my cheeks are red. I don't seem to be wearing a shirt. Someone's fingers, from the top knuckles upwards, are visible just below my neck, but the rest of the hand is cut off by the bottom edge of the photograph. The fingernails are torn and dirty. There are only three fingers on the hand. Upon closer inspection, the wall behind me is not blurred: it is ruined, the paper torn and dirtied, the uneven plaster beneath lined and raked as if by something sharp. Like nails. Or claws.

• Another blank page. But this one has small bits of adhesive dotted on the paper, as if whatever photograph was there has been hastily removed.

• The final photograph is perhaps the most disturbing of all, yet the least clear in terms of what is going on. The photographer has stepped forward, must be standing on the doorstep, so only a part of the doorframe is visible. At the end of the grimy hallway, there are two figures. Both are facing away from the black door, and from the camera. One of the figures is the familiar thin, lanky creature from one of the previous shots. Its shoulders are hunched; its lean thighs are clenched, as if it's been caught in the act of taking a step. Holding its hand is another, smaller figure. A scrawny boy, aged perhaps fourteen years old. The boy is naked. I recognise myself from the birthmark behind my right knee: a small, dark circular stain. The muscles in my body are tensed; I can see that even from the grainy, unfocused shot. Beyond the two figures, just about visible in the darkness at the end of the hallway, is my father. His nude body is a vague pinkish blur, but his face is a little easier to make out: a small, hazy oval in the shadows. His arms are crossed at the wrist over his pelvis. He is gripping something in his fist but I don't know what it is. His eyes are small and mean, and he is grinning.

I close the album and put it on the bed. Get up and walk to the mirror. Reflected there, in the glass, I see something other than the familiar room where I spent my childhood evenings, fighting back nightmares.

I see a black door in the wall, its letterbox stuffed with dead leaves and its gold handle and knocker slightly tarnished. As I watch, the door opens. A long, thin, pale three-fingered hand bends around the frame. I stare at the ragged nails, the blood and dirt I know is crusted beneath them, and I remember.

He was always there, in my life, ever since I was six years old. For most of the time he stayed in the background, but sometimes he put on a mask and entered the frame, unable to stay out of view. I'm still not sure who he was, but my father brought him into our home, and some kind of transaction took place. My birthmark is a stamp, a barcode; it marks me out as belonging to him. Bought and paid for long ago, before the first photograph was even taken.

Each time I was taken there, to the house with the black door, I came out with something missing. The memory of what happened inside, yes, but also something else: a small part of me, sliced away. I think Shelley Cork got to see what was in there, too, but she never came back out. I suspect that my father led her through that black door and left her there, a plaything for whatever resides at the end of that dirty hallway.

I shift my gaze and stare at the door in the mirror. My face resembles that of my father, at the age that I am now. A non-identical reflection; like the left hand swapping places with the right. It does not fit. It should not be there, where it does not belong.

I glance again at the black door. It has always been waiting for me to return. The long, thin hand slips away, retreating back inside, but the door does not shut. It will never shut, not until I go back inside to take back what is mine.

To reclaim the things I left behind and stick those missing photographs back in the album.

KAIJU

DIVING DEEP, SOMETHING LARGE MOVES *and writhes with the currents, heading into the comforting darkness. The waters become cold, the water pressure increases. A sleek, muscled body drives on, speeding ever downwards, moving fast towards the bottom of everything.*

Jeff pulled up at the kerb and stared out of the side window at the remains of his house. The army took down the roadblocks a few days ago, the useable highways were being patrolled by the police and the Territorial Army, and things were slowly making their way back towards some kind of normality.

He didn't want to leave the car. He felt as if it offered him some kind of protective bubble from the world. Not in any literal sense, of course—nobody felt safe now, not after what happened—but inside the car, behind a layer of metal and glass, he could at least compartmentalise his thoughts.

There was no point in staying here, though. He had no choice but to get out. He needed to be sure there were no survivors.

He shifted his gaze to the windscreen and watched a young woman picking her way through the rubble a few yards up ahead. She was dressed in a blue boiler suit, like the kind worn by staff on the factory floor where he used to work, and her hair was pulled back severely from her face. Her pale cheeks were smudged with dirt. Her tiny white hands looked steady enough, but her gait was ungainly as she moved carefully through the broken bricks and shattered timbers that had once formed a home—presumably hers, or that of someone she knew.

Jeff felt like crying. He had lost so much. Everybody had. He didn't know a single person who'd remained untouched by the events of the past three weeks. When that thing attacked, it brought with it only destruction. Like a biblical plague, it wiped out everything in its path.

That *thing*...the beast...the monster...

Thinking of it now, he felt stupid. It was a child's word used to describe something he struggled to label in an adult world. Everything changed the day it arrived; even the rules of physics were twisted out of shape, along with the precarious geometry of his own existence.

When he was a boy, he'd loved reading comics and watching films about monsters. Now that he was a man, and he had seen the proof that monsters really existed, he could not even begin to fathom what his younger self had found so fascinating about them.

He opened the door and got out of the car. Night was falling, but it was still light enough to see clearly. There was a slight chill in the air. The woman was closer now to his position, and she wasn't as young as he'd initially thought. Middle-aged: possibly in her early forties. The mud on her face had clouded her features, at first hiding the wrinkles and the layers of anguish that were now visible.

"Have you seen them?" She approached him as she spoke, stumbling a little as she crossed onto the footpath. He saw that the heel of one of her shoes—the left one—had snapped off during her travels. The woman hadn't even noticed.

"I'm sorry?"

"We all are...we're all sorry. But have you seen them? My

children."

He clenched his fists. Moments like these, situations in which he could smell and taste and just about touch someone else's loss, made him nervous. He felt like a little boy again, reading about mythical creatures from a large hardback book.

"No. No, I haven't."

"They're still alive. Somewhere." She glanced around, at the wreckage of the neighbourhood. Her eyes were wide. Her lips were slack. "They let me come back here to try and find them. They were in the cellar when it...when it hit. The Storm..."

That's what they called it: the Storm. The name seemed fitting. He couldn't remember who'd first coined the term: probably some newspaper reporter.

"I..." He stopped there, unable to think of anything that might help the woman come to terms with her loss.

"I got out, but they stayed down there. The army truck took me away—they wouldn't let me go back for them. They were trapped, you see...by the rubble. The Storm trapped them inside, underneath. I have to find them."

She reached out and grabbed his arm. He could barely feel her grip, despite her knuckles whitening as her fingers tightened around his bicep. "Could you help me look for them?" Her smile, when it struggled to the surface, was horrible. Jeff thought he'd never seen an expression so empty.

"I have to...I have things to do. This was my house." He pointed to the pile of bricks and timbers and the scattered glass shards; the piles of earth; the pit formed by a single foot of the Storm.

"We were neighbours?" She peered at him, trying to focus. "Before it happened?"

"I guess so." He'd never seen her before in his life. This woman was a stranger, but they were all supposed to be connected by their shared tragedy. Jeff had never felt that way. He was alone with his ghosts.

They stood there for another moment, as if glued together by some sticky strands of time, and then he pulled away. Her arm remained hanging there, the fingers of her hand curling over empty air.

"My children..."

He looked into her eyes and saw nothing, not even an echo of her pain. She was stripped bare, rendered down to nothing but this mindless search for things that were no longer here. He couldn't tell her; she wouldn't be told. She needed to discover the truth for herself.

"Good luck," he said, and he meant it.

Jeff walked away, heading towards the ragged hole in the earth where his house had once stood, the great footprint of the beast that had once passed this way. He wished he'd seen it happen. It must have been an amazing sight, to see the buildings flattened by the gigantic beast as it charged through the neighbourhood and towards the city.

He heard the woman's scuffling footsteps behind him as she moved away. He wished he had it in him to help her. He hoped she would find her children alive, but doubted she ever would. Not even the bodies would remain. Not even bloodstains.

The Storm came, and that was all. There was no reason for its arrival. It wasn't like the old movies he'd seen as a kid, where an atomic detonation or the constant experimentation of mankind caused a rift in the earth or a disturbance in the atmosphere, and out stumbled a stop-motion nightmare. No, it was nothing like that. The Storm came, it destroyed whatever it encountered, and it went away again, sated.

They were unable to fight it. The authorities didn't know what to do; the army and navy and air force were at a loss: none of their weapons had any effect on the Storm. So they waited it out, hoping the thing would either wear itself out and tire of the rampage, or move on, crossing the border into another country. Fingers hovered over the buttons of nuclear launch systems. Members of Parliament voted in secret chambers. The nation prepared for a great and terrible sacrifice.

He remembered those first surprisingly clear pieces of footage transmitted on the Internet, and then again on the news channels: HD-quality CCTV pictures of some great lizard-like beast emerging from the shadows on the coast, a B-movie come to life. But this was not a man in a suit, or a too-crisp CGI image. It was colossal, the height of two tower blocks, one standing on top of the other. Its arm span was a half mile across, but it barely needed to stretch them so far to tear down a church, a town hall, a factory warehouse... Bullets and bombs simply bounced off its thick, plated hide to create more damage to the surrounding area. Its call was the trumpet of Armageddon. When it opened its mouth to roar, the sound was unlike anything humanity had heard before.

Nobody knew what the creature was, where it came from, why it appeared. The scientists mumbled in jargon, talked about tectonic plates, seismic events, and then finally, they went quiet. They locked themselves into deep underground laboratories to try and invent something that would kill the thing.

And then...then it went away, slinking back into the ocean, the waves covering it like a blanket. The sea bubbled. Ships capsized. The coastal barriers fell. The Storm passed.

But the Storm could return at any time. They all knew this, but it went unspoken. There were celebrations, the blockades came down, people started to rebuild what had been ravaged. But somewhere back in the shadows, or under the dark waters, the Storm waited. Perhaps it even watched.

Jeff walked across the roughly turned earth, his boots hard and solid as he made his way towards the hole in the ground. When he reached it, he went down onto his knees and peered over the rim. It was deep, with standing water gathered at its base and in each of the toe prints. There was no sign of a body, or of body parts. His family was wiped out, deleted, removed without trace from the face of the earth.

He smiled, gritting his teeth.

As a boy he'd loved monsters. As a man, he wasn't so sure how he felt.

If it were not for the Storm, he would have been forced to think of some other way to dispose of them, but the monster had answered his desperate prayers and come to cleanse him, to remove the evidence of his crimes.

He wondered...

If he hoped hard enough, wished for long enough, might it come back? There were other people he wanted to get rid of. It was a nice thought, but he knew it was a fantasy. The situation had nothing to do with him; it was simply a handy coincidence. Even now, it amused him to think something this absurd had saved him from being found out. It was as if one of those childhood comic books had come to life.

Jeff got to his feet and moved slowly away from the ruins. The breeze turned into a light wind, and it whipped up a mass of litter, sending papers and packets and scraps of material scampering into the gutter. Jeff watched them as they tussled. He remembered the way his family struggled: Katherine and the girls, fighting for their sad little lives. It was like watching a movie, only less real. The actors didn't even look like the people they were trying to portray.

They'd never looked like his family, those actors. The woman he'd married, the daughters he'd fathered, were at some point replaced by strangers. That was why they had to go. It had all seemed so clear, and then, without thinking, he'd done it: he had ended them. There was no memory of planning or running through it all in his mind. There was only the act itself, and the mess left behind.

The wind died down. The litter went still. He smelled old fires and diesel fumes. He tasted bitterness at the back of his throat. Something huge loomed against the horizon, its form unclear, fluttering and unstable.

Jeff walked back to the car, climbed inside, turned on the engine, and waited. He watched the woman as she made her way across the street, towards yet another ruined house. He smiled. Inside his head, he heard the voice of the Storm.

The roaming woman sat down in the rubble, staring at the ground. She clenched and unclenched her hands and then started rooting in the dirt, as if she might find her lost children there, somewhere beneath the disturbed topsoil. He imagined her brushing away gravel to see a face staring up at her, eyes closed, lips sealed shut on a silent scream.

Clouds moved behind her, shifting across the low red sky. Something dark shimmered beyond them, like a promise straining to be fulfilled. He thought of giant butterfly wings, and then of the opening mouth of the Storm.

Jeff started the car but waited a few moments—still watching the woman—before driving away. He didn't turn on the radio. All they ever talked about was the Storm.

As he headed down the road, towards some unidentified place he'd never been before, he thought about this new world and wondered how everyone would cope with the way things were now, the changes happening in the wake of the monster. Jeff had stepped through the veil, but the rest of the world followed behind him.

He drove all night, and then he stopped the car in a lonely place to sit and look up at the sky. Trees stirred like wraiths against the breezy evening. The stars pulsed, the darkness bulged, threatening to burst open like a ripe melon, and he tried to catch a glimpse of the old world, the one they'd all left behind. After a long time, he gave up trying.

And at the bottom of the sea, curled up among the old wrecks in a long, deep, nameless trench, something yawns and blinks its eyes before drifting back into a deep, soundless slumber. It dreams of screams and bloodshed and finds comfort in the sweet memory of Man's fear.

IT ONLY HURTS ON THE WAY OUT

KURT HAS BEEN OUT OF hospital for over a week by the time Marc finally comes to visit.

His half-brother skulks into the room like a kid with a dirty secret, hands stuffed into the pockets of his baggy jeans, baseball cap pulled down over his eyes as if he's a street corner gangsta.

"He wouldn't go away," says Sally, in her usual blunt manner. "I told him to fuck off, but he wouldn't."

"It's okay," says Kurt, sitting up in bed and switching off the television. "He's here now."

She gives him an odd look—one that's poised somewhere between a smile and a frown—and before he can finish reading the expression, she's left the room, shutting the door firmly behind her.

"She's a bitch." Marc shuffles to the end of the bed, taking off his cap and holding it in both hands in front of his crotch. "A right piece of work."

"Yeah, yeah, and according to her you're a thieving junkie bastard, so what's new?"

Marc smiles. He's forgotten to put in his dentures, so the gap where his four front teeth used to be looks black in the dim room: a cheap special effect from a bad stage show.

"What is it, Marc? You haven't even asked how I am. For your information, I'm tired. I have to rest. The doctor said so." Kurt rubs at the bandages on his wrists without realising until the wounds begin to ache. It's become something he does now. He wonders if he'll keep it up, as a habit, even when the dressings come off.

"Still hurts, eh?"

He nods. Sighs. Rubs.

"Did you do it lengthways, like you're meant to if you really want to die?"

Kurt says nothing.

"They say if you do it the other way—across the wrist—it's just a cry for help. Not a real attempt to die, but an attention-seeking thing."

"Who does? Who says?"

Marc shrugs. "I dunno. People on the telly, I suppose. In films, an' that."

"What the fuck do you want, Marc?"

Marc sits on the edge of the bed. The old wooden frame creaks; the mattress sags beneath his not exactly inconsiderable weight. He isn't fat but he's broad and solid, like their father used to be. "It's back."

Kurt shifts into a more comfortable position and reaches behind his head to adjust the pillows. "What is?" But he knows; of course he does. He could always read Marc so damned easily. He tries to think of a way to ignore what's being said, but he can't. There's no way out of this conversation.

"The little red house. It's come back. I told you it would, didn't I?"

"What have you been smoking?"

"I've been up all night with some quality weed. But that isn't the issue. What matters is that it's back. In a different place, of course, but it's back. Like I always knew it would be. Just like the old man promised."

Kurt wishes that his half-brother would go away and never come back. He ran off so many times when they were kids that they lost count, and he was often brought home again by tired-looking policemen with stern expressions. They usually found him in squats or homeless shelters or sleeping in the bins behind abandoned buildings. He hasn't done that since he was a teenager, though. There's no need now that he's grown up; man-children like Marc can do what the hell they want and never have to run away. It's only people like Kurt who can never escape the realities of their existence.

"We've been through all this before. There is no little red house. It was a drug dream, a hallucination. It doesn't exist. Never did."

Kurt can hear Sally in another room, opening and closing the cupboard doors, then slamming pots and pans onto the kitchen worktops. He can imagine her face, the sagging skin, the tired, tired eyes, the folds in her neck. She was never what anyone would call beautiful, but recently she's turned ugly. Or maybe he's just started to see her as she really is, as she always has been.

"It exists, man. I saw it again, last night." Marc glances at his watch.

He shakes his head and starts to rise from the bed.

"Wanna come with me? I can show it to you this time. We can go inside."

Kurt is never sure afterwards why he didn't just throw Marc out and go back to sleep.

The words simply came out of his mouth: "Yeah, okay. Why not."

Later he will come to realise that part of it was because he didn't want to spend another hour alone with Sally in her current mood, and the last thing he wanted to eat was her angry cooking.

Beyond that, he can never be sure what motivated him to follow Marc out into the cold night in search of an old family myth.

Outside, the streetlight on the corner is flickering. It's been doing so for over a week and the council still hasn't turned up to fix it.

"She'll be okay," says Marc. "She'll get over it when you come back with a cool story about the little red house."

"So tell me again why you didn't take a photo of it on your phone." He's trying to change the subject. Sally's rage—and its frequency—is the last thing he wants to discuss. He's been trying to get away from it for what seems like forever.

"I did. I took loads. They just didn't turn out. I don't think it can be photographed. I doubt everyone can even see it, just a few chosen people."

"So you're one of the special ones, eh?"

Marc's head snaps around on his broad neck. "I didn't say that. I just think that maybe...maybe you have to be damaged in a certain way to be able to see it, that's all." His eyes narrow, as if he's waiting for an inevitable put-down.

"Okay," says Kurt, feeling a familiar and unwelcome sense of pity for the younger man.

Marc has not lived a good life. Their father jumped off a bridge to his death in front of the boy when he was eleven, and Marc has never known his real mother. She was just some whore their father made pregnant: one of the many lost souls he kept on a leash as part of his pathetic little suburban cult.

"Where is it?"

Marc leads the way, moving through the patch of trees on the corner of Lyric Street and hopping over a fence into a parking area Kurt doesn't recognise. There are only two or three old-looking vehicles parked in spaces, as if they've been left there and forgotten. "It's down by the river," he says, not even turning around. "That half-demolished pedestrian tunnel, with the old bypass over the top."

"What? Through there?"

Marc stops and glances to his right; his face is in profile, but it's too dark to make out the features. "No, it's inside. In the tunnel." He continues at a quicker pace, as if he fears that Kurt might change his mind now that they are so close.

It doesn't take them long to reach the tunnel. The concrete is old and cracked, with layers of graffiti painted over its surface. Parts of the tunnel have fallen away, creating holes in the structure. The steel reinforcement rods are visible in places, a crosshatching of rusted bones.

"I've never liked it down here," says Kurt, wishing once again that he hadn't come. "It's always had an air of danger... Remember years ago, when that old lady was chased by some weirdo on the other side of the tunnel? She said her attacker was wearing a pig-faced mask. Weird shit."

Marc is silent as he pulls aside the plastic barriers erected by workmen, making space for them to pass through. He looks up at the unused road that passes overhead and then back into the darkness of the tunnel mouth. "This way," he says, softly. "I can't wait for you to see." Then he moves slowly inside.

Kurt steps over steel rods, shards of crumbling concrete, and the kind of tape the police use to seal off crime scenes. He stumbles once, grabbing hold of the rotting tunnel wall for support, and is looking down at his feet so he fails to get a glimpse inside the tunnel until it's too late to turn back.

There it is, up ahead, halfway along the tunnel's length: the little red house.

"Do you see it?"

Kurt nods. He can't find the words. He thought he was here to humour Marc, but it turns out that he's going to see something he didn't even believe was real.

"Well, do you?"

He nods again, and then croaks rather than speaks a response.

Marc is grinning. "I told you. I told you it was real."

The little red house is made out of ancient timber boards and painted a dark shade of red. Crimson, really, like horror movie blood. It has two stories, four windows and a door. The little red house stands as tall as Kurt; it is narrow and crooked, like a cartoon abode. There are no lights on in the windows. The front door is shut.

"Can we go now?"

"Can we, hell. I want to go inside."

"No...we won't fit. It's too small."

"Just a quick look. The door might not even open. I just want to see if it does." Marc steps forward, reaching out to grasp the door handle. Kurt hasn't even realised they are still walking forward; hasn't understood how close they are to the little red house. They seem to have floated to the threshold.

"I don't know about this."

"Yes. Let's do it." Marc's hand closes over the handle.

Kurt knows the door will open before it even does. It was always meant to.

In another version of this story, it is locked and they turn around and go home, experience productive lives and have children whom they tell about this night, turning it into a fable, a scary story to keep the kids away from dangerous places.

But in this version, something else happens:

The door cracks open, bleeding darkness from within. Marc pushes gently and it swings slowly inward, revealing a dark, narrow hallway that looks far too long to be enclosed within this tiny little house. The image shudders as if it is unstable, a scene shot on old film stock. Found footage projected over the backdrop of reality.

"Come on," says Marc. "I'll go first."

Kurt doesn't want to go inside, but he can't make his feet stop moving, nor can he force his body to turn away. That floating sensation again: making up ground without being aware of moving. Before he knows what is happening, he's stepping over the threshold, following his half-brother inside this impossible place. The image stabilises, becoming more real. The hallway solidifies. It seems to stretch on for miles.

"This is gonna be so cool," whispers Marc, as the door snickers shut behind them.

Inside it's like a cheap theme park attraction. The floor is uneven; the walls are painted with lumpy glow-in-the-dark paint that is also red. There are picture frames but with no pictures in them, all painted red. Bare-board floors. Plaster walls. Skirting boards are torn and fractured. Everything is painted the same shade of red.

"This isn't right. It's too big in here..." Kurt is walking with his hands held out before him, ready to ward off whatever might come hurtling out of the darkness up ahead.

"No, not too big," says Marc. "Too long. It's too long in here. Just one long hallway..."

He's right. There are no doors leading off the hallway; no stairs to take them up or down. It's just a seemingly endless hallway, an impossible passage leading into a twitching, pregnant darkness, a little like the mouth of a cave.

"I don't like this," says Marc. "Not one bit."

That's when the music starts. Just like that, as if a switch has been thrown.

The two men stop moving and stand there, listening. The music is coming from far away, but the song is one they both know. Lilting, melancholy, a familiar melody but slightly out of tune. It sounds as if it's being played on an old-fashioned gramophone, or perhaps a fairground calliope, located in another building along some quiet street nearby.

"*The Wizard of Oz*," says Marc.

"It's 'Somewhere Over the Rainbow'," adds Kurt. "Judy Garland...but that isn't her voice singing."

Their father's favourite film. He used to play the soundtrack recording all the time when they were kids. Whenever his friends came around, the ones that venerated him as some kind of spiritual leader, he would play it then too. They would all sit on the floor in a circle with their eyes closed and listen.

The singing voice is horrible, at once child-like and as ancient as the hills, with each syllable containing a hint of terrible things once seen and done. A prisoner lamenting in a dark cell, or a lonely child awaiting some terrible event.

"I think I dreamed this once," says Marc. "This exact thing. The song and everything. Or is it a memory, one that I can't quite reach?"

"What happened...what happened in the dream?"

"I don't know. Maybe I never woke up from it. Maybe we're both still inside my dream."

Kurt turns around, but he can see nothing apart from the red-tinged darkness of the hallway behind him. The door has gone; the walls angle inwards to a point. It's a false perspective, surely, but a terrifying one.

The music moves farther away, as if the singer is retreating at a slow pace, or the gramophone is being pulled along in the other direction.

"We need to get out of here."

Marc shuffles on the spot. "Which way? I feel like we've been turned around and backwards is forwards is backwards."

Kurt feels the same way. Now that Marc has verbalised the notion, it describes exactly how he's been feeling since they entered the little red house: utterly without direction.

"How long have we even been in here, Marc?"

"I don't know..." His voice is cracking; fear is pouring in. He sounds older, or in pain. He sounds like their father.

"I think you need to wake up from that dream now."

At the sound of his words, the music ends, mid-verse. From far away, a slow thudding, like heavy footsteps, starts to move in their direction.

"You need to wake up and get us the fuck out of here."

The footsteps begin to run.

"Please, Marc, wake up. Now."

Marc starts to cry.

"Wake the fuck up!"

"I can't. I don't even know if I'm still asleep."

Kurt shuts his eyes as tight as he can. Perhaps if he pretends to be asleep he can wake them both up instead. Or at the very least, whatever is now speeding their way might not see them and pass on by.

He remembers what he'd done when he was a child, afraid of the dark and the soft chanting from downstairs as his father's disciples offered up their prayers. Squeezing shut his eyes and thinking, *If I can't see the monster, the monster can't see me...*

He strains harder, forcing shut his eyes so hard that the muscles begin to ache.

"Kurt...I'm scared..."

Harder...

When Kurt opens his eyes he is alone, lying on his side on the ground in the decrepit pedestrian tunnel, one hand resting in a shallow puddle of dirty water. The little red house has gone. There is no sign of Marc.

He can remember very little after entering the house. There is a dim recollection of trying to go to sleep, and then of falling into a darkness that felt like an ocean. Music.

What did we see?

He can recall an endless hallway without doors and the panicked attempt to either fall asleep or wake up.

He struggles to his feet and walks slowly to the concrete tunnel's shabby entrance. Diffuse light is seeping gradually back into the world. It's still late, but soon it will be too early.

Where did that thought come from, and what does it even mean?

His head is full of strange, unformed ideas; shadows flit and flicker in the alleyways of his brain. Kurt knows that he encountered something fundamentally bad in the little red house, but he has no idea what it was. Just a vague presence, a thing that cast its shadow over him and then moved on, leaving him changed, different.

It was a cloud occluding the sun, a dark wing drawn across the moon.

He looks down at his arms. The dressings are gone, the wounds clean and healed. Faint scars make circles around his wrists. He can't even remember why he tried to kill himself, or if indeed it was nothing more than a cry for help, as Marc had suggested.

All he knows is the blade didn't feel too bad going in; it only hurt on the way out. He wishes he could tell Marc, but the time for such talk is long gone.

When he gets home, he creeps quietly inside and goes to the bedroom.

The bed is empty; Sally must have decided to sleep in the other room to punish him for following Marc and his idiot imaginings. She's always doing that—dishing out some form of punishment for imagined slights.

He slips off his clothes and slides into bed, beneath the cool sheets. The room is dark but he can see clearly, as if the dark is now his light. He wonders what else has changed; how the world will look when he wakes in the morning, born again into a place that he can only barely recognise.

His eyes drift shut and he feels sleep dragging him down.

He keeps opening his eyes, but they are too heavy to remain that way.

Through the twitching lids, he sees the little red house appear in the corner of his room. It looks like a projected image, flickering, insubstantial. One of the upstairs lights is on.

He hears a song that sounds at once familiar and completely alien—even obscene. It reminds him of childhood, but the feeling isn't a comfortable one, or in any way nostalgic.

Is that Marc calling his name over and over, or is he simply re-entering the dream that he now realises was always waiting for him along that long red hallway in the little red house?

Later, he wakes into a silence that feels like a physical weight. His limbs are heavy, the muscles having to work hard to propel him across the room. It feels a lot like swimming.

The little red house is not there, but still he can feel its presence.

He realises that it will always be near him now that he has seen it, hovering just beyond the edge of his vision. He will see it again, but its emergence will be unannounced.

Sally is in the kitchen making breakfast. He opens his mouth to speak but only the song comes out—grainy, as if it is emerging from a distant, damaged speaker.

Sally doesn't turn around. She can't hear him. Her hair is streaked with grey; her body is thin. She has not aged well in his absence.

Kurt has no idea how long he has been away.

He reaches out a hand and grabs her shoulder. She twitches and drops her weight to one side. When he raises the other hand, it's painted red. Just like the house: small, red, and not quite there.

He smiles and lets the song draw closer, becoming clearer. The little red house beckons to him from somewhere far away. If he does things right and performs certain as-yet-unknown rituals, he's sure that he can go there again, and this time the house, and whatever dwells within it, might let him stay for good.

He'll get to see Marc again.

The little red house might let him and Sally dwell there forever and change them into the people he's always wanted them to be: the kind of people who get to live somewhere over the rainbow, in a little red house with an impossible hallway containing all the possibilities denied them in the past.

He takes Sally in his little red arms and holds her so tightly that even when the look of surprise vanishes from her face and she begins to scream and struggle against him, there is no chance of her ever breaking free.

It took a little while for the truth to sink in, but now he knows what it is he'd failed to understand about the house all along: once you've been inside, you can never really leave.

KILL ALL MONSTERS

TWO OR THREE MILES SOUTH of Sheffield they pulled off the M1 motorway and into the badly-lit car park of a grubby little roadside restaurant. Squat buildings huddled in the darkness, separated by narrow patches of overgrown wasteland. The road was narrow; the aged asphalt surface was cracked and blistered.

The woman glanced at the clock on the dashboard; it was two-thirty a.m. The child was asleep in the back, snoring softly. The woman reached across and clasped the man's hand on the steering wheel. Darkness pressed against the windows and the sides of the car. Metal creaked. The engine cooled.

"Here?" she said, softly. "Should we risk it?"

The man nodded. "We need to eat. Something to drink. We can't just keep driving." His gaze was locked dead ahead, focused at a point a few yards from the windscreen. There wasn't much to see but he was staring intensely: a high white-rendered concrete wall, a row of grey plastic bins, a pile of black rubbish bags with their tops knotted.

"I'll wake the child," she said, opening the car door. The interior light came on, flickered. The inrush of cold air from outside was like an unexpected kiss. It lifted her; she felt unfettered from the small, claustrophobic world inside the car. She could barely hear the traffic from the motorway, just the occasional hypnotic swish of hot rubber on smooth tarmac.

She walked around to the back of the car and opened the rear door. The child was lying across the back seat, her long, thin legs stretched out on the upholstery. Light from the small, jittery overhead bulb pooled around her face and gathered in her long blonde hair.

"Time to get up," she said, reaching inside to give the child's arm a shake. "We're here."

The child stirred. Sat up, blinking. She rubbed at her cheeks, scratched her head. "I'm hungry," she said.

"I know. You're always hungry." The woman smiled and stepped back, moving in a crouch away from the car to let the child climb out. She caught sight of her face in the wing mirror. There were dark bags around her eyes, but the bruises on her cheek had faded to look like smudges of dirt. Her long sleeves hid the scratches on her arms.

It's okay, she thought. *You're fine, now.*

The car park wasn't busy. Only a handful of vehicles sat in white-lined spaces. It was too late for the dinner traffic and too early for the breakfast crowd.

The man got out of the car, waited, and then locked the doors. He walked ahead of them, towards the island of light that was the restaurant, and paused, holding open the double doors until they caught up.

"Just be cool," said the woman. "Be cool."

The man nodded, smiling. *If he's still able to smile*, she thought, *things can't be too bad.*

They walked inside and sat down at a table in the window. It always had to be in the window; the man claimed that he hated feeling hemmed in, and that being able to look outside helped to calm him.

"Is it waitress service?" He picked up a salt cellar and shook it. Tiny grains of salt made a small conical pile on the red plastic tablecloth, an unstable construction that might collapse at any given moment.

"I don't know," said the woman, afraid for some reason that the little hill of salt might crumble and provoke an outburst from the man. "I'll go and see." She stood quickly and eagerly and walked over to the checkout. A bored young girl, barely out of her teens, was flicking through a magazine and chewing a wad of gum.

"Excuse me," said the woman. "Is it self-service?"

"Yeah," said the young girl, without even looking up. Her dark red fingernails flashed as she quickly turned the pages of the magazine.

The woman returned to the table. She didn't sit back down. She knew the man hated the kind of impatient "fuck-you" attitude demonstrated by the girl. It was a trigger. "It's get-your-own. The food's over there." She used her thumb to point without looking back towards the checkout.

The man nodded. "Okay. That's fine."

"I'll get the stuff. What do you need?" She was aware that her question could be taken in one of an infinite number of ways.

The man glanced up. His lips were pressed tightly together; they were thin and pale. "I'll have a sandwich," he said. His lips regained their natural colour as he moved them. "Tuna or ham. Something like that, you know what I like... And a coffee. Black. No sugar."

The woman nodded. "What about you?"

The child was staring out of the window. "Can I have a donut?"

"Yes," said the woman. "And some milk?"

"Yeah, milk."

The woman waited a few seconds more, just to make sure they were done, and then she walked over towards the food displays. She grabbed a tray from the pile—squares of thin brown plastic made to look like wood—and walked along the refrigerated display cases. She took a tuna and sweet corn sandwich on white bread for the man, a fresh cream donut for the girl, and a cheese salad for herself. She poured two cups of coffee into cardboard cups at the machine and took a carton of milk from a chiller box next to the checkout.

For a moment she felt like crying, so she stood there and waited for it to pass. There was a heavy weight in her chest, pressing against her ribs. She closed her eyes and took a deep breath. Then, once the sensation had passed, she opened her eyes again.

She paid the cashier without speaking. It was better that way; she didn't want to communicate with someone who seemed so hideously empty. She knew exactly what the man would have done, and was thankful that she'd been the one to get the food.

She returned to the table with the tray of provisions. The man tore the wrapper off his sandwich and wolfed it down. The child nibbled at her donut, slowly licking the cream from her fingers. The woman picked at her salad. It tasted flat, like fake food from a cheap window display.

There were not many other customers in the restaurant, just a few scattered diners. Most of them were alone, but two silent couples sat diagonally opposite each other across the room. The geometry of their positioning bothered the woman, but she didn't know why. Her life these days was filled with such random and inexplicable fears.

"We have to go soon," she said, glancing at the man.

He was staring at the child.

"I said we'll have to go soon."

Please notice me, she thought. *Tell me I'm more than just your babysitter.*

He looked over in her direction. His eyes were wide and wet, as if he were fighting tears. "I know," he said, and smiled sadly. "We can go soon enough. Just give me a minute." His lean, handsome face seemed to promise more than he could ever give.

The lighting in the place was giving her a headache. It was too bright; harsh and unrealistic. She imagined it was not dissimilar to the lighting in hospital morgues, where corpses were dissected beneath cold white bulbs.

Panic welled up inside her. She looked again at the man. He was no longer looking at the child, or out of the window; he was watching the other people in the room. One of his hands was a fist on the table. The other had balled up the wrapper from his sandwich. There were crumbs on his jacket cuff, but he'd failed to notice them.

"Nearly finished?" she said to the child, a sense of urgency causing her to speak too loudly.

The child had cream smeared on her upper lip. She licked it off. "Almost," she said, distracted.

Behind her, someone got up and walked across the quiet room. The footsteps were heavy; they belonged to a man. She turned around and glanced at him. He was young—perhaps in his late twenties—and wearing fashionable clothes with designer labels. He carried an iPad in one hand. The light on the machine was flashing.

These were exactly the kind of things that tended to set the man off: people in designer clothing, flashy techno toys, a look of arrogance, a smile of dismissal, an educated accent...the list was endless. And there were new triggers to add to the list every day.

She looked over at the man. His eyes were dry. They were hungry. It was happening again and there was nothing she could do to stop it.

"Don't," she said, reaching across the table to grab hold of his hand—the fisted one. "Not here. Not this time. Not in front of the child. Let's just leave."

When he turned towards her, his face was flushed; his cheeks were mottled. His lips were damp with spit. He was grinding his teeth. "When?"

She squeezed his hand. "Not long now. Just hang on for a little while longer, until she's finished eating." She could see the threat of violence in his eyes, as if a moment was suspended there, frozen forever. "Just be good."

He closed his eyes and bowed his head. "Monsters," he muttered, more to himself than anyone else. "They're fucking everywhere. I see them wherever we go."

"I know, baby." She looked again at the young man who had passed by. He was vanishing into a door marked "toilets."

The man's shoulders were hitching. He was ready to blow. "Gotta stop them all...stop all the damn monsters."

She had to make a quick decision, to prevent the situation from becoming even worse. She remembered the time when he'd assaulted two bystanders and wrecked a petrol station forecourt, trying to get at a middle-aged businesswoman in the passenger seat of a Ford Mondeo. All the attention it had drawn; their blurred CCTV photographs in the paper; their mad rush to change vehicles so that the police couldn't track them down.

They'd been on the move ever since, driving at night, sleeping all day in cheap hotel rooms, eating their meals at overly-lit, lonely little all-night places like this one. Crossing the country in a succession of different vehicles, each one picked up cheap at cash-only used car depots. But England was a small country; soon they would run out of road. Then what would they do, simply turn around and run the other way?

She still didn't understand how they'd never been caught.

We're riding our luck; surely it must run out soon.

Surely...

"Okay," she said, softly but firmly. "Do it now. Do it quickly. He's in the bathroom. Nobody will see."

The man looked up, smiled, and got to his feet.

She flinched when he moved, and hated herself for it. Each time this happened she felt another piece of herself breaking away. Sometimes she thought the only reason she stayed with the man was because if she left, the rest of her would flake off like scabs of rust and there'd be nothing left. This relationship, this twisted dynamic, was the only thing keeping her alive.

The man walked quickly and soundlessly across the restaurant—it never failed to chill her, the way in which such a large man could move with that kind of quiet grace. She tried to pretend that she didn't see him quickly grab a knife from the cutlery tray on his way to the bathroom.

Nobody even noticed him as he followed the other man through the doorway. The door swung silently on its hinges.

"Come on," she said to the child. "Eat up now. We have to go." The thought hit her that she could stand up now and run, get away. Leave him behind. But where would she go, and who would she run to? She had nothing; there was nobody else…just the man and the child. Without them both she would somehow feel less complete, less of a real human being. She'd been doing this so long that it had become what defined her. She belonged here, with these people, in these places.

It didn't take long. It never did.

The man reappeared less than thirty seconds later. The door hadn't even stopped swinging. His eyes were shining, his jacket was undone, and as he approached the table, she could see that his knuckles were bright red and raw. They'd be bruised in the morning. She would have to find somewhere on the road to get some ice to stop the swelling.

He stood at the side of the table with a faraway look in his eyes, swaying ever so slightly on his heels. There were a few spots of blood on his jacket sleeve. He didn't seem able to focus, not yet. It always took a minute or two for him to snap back into the moment.

She wondered where he'd left the knife. Or had he slipped it into his pocket to carry with him? They were blunt, those knives; it would be difficult to cause any real damage. That's what she told herself. That's what she hoped.

"Back to the car. Now." She grabbed the child's arm and pulled her gently to her feet. The remains of the donut fell onto the floor. They moved towards the door, the three of them together—a family. The man was once again in front. He pushed open the glass doors and held them while the woman and the child went through, out into the night.

She raised her eyebrows as she brushed past him. He nodded, confirming that the red mist had cleared. He looked like he was just about to say something—*I love you?*—but then he closed his mouth and looked away, ashamed.

Even now, after all this time, he felt shame. That was part of the reason she still loved him, and why she thought that he could be saved.

The air outside was cold; the temperature had dropped dramatically during the short time they'd been inside.

"I didn't even finish my donut," said the child, pouting.

They hurried across the car park and waited until the man unlocked the car. The woman's breath was a fine white mist. She bundled the child into the back seat and strapped her in. They might have to drive at speed; she didn't want to risk the child being injured if they had an accident, like last time. A few weeks ago, after a visit to an all-night supermarket, he'd run the car off the road and into a drainage ditch. She'd told the doctors in A&E that the child had fallen off her bike. She didn't think they'd believed her, but they helped the child anyway, patching her up and sending them both away with orders to return for a check-up in a week's time.

By the time she climbed into the passenger seat, the man was already at the wheel, gunning the engine.

"Will it ever end?" he said, staring through the windscreen. "I don't think I can keep doing this. There's too many of them. I'm just one man...one man...I can't do it all. I have to stop putting you through this—both of you. You don't deserve this..."

She placed a hand on his thigh. The muscles there were rock hard. She rubbed the dry palm of her hand against the rough leg of his jeans. "I know," she said. "We just have to keep on hoping that the next one will be the last."

He closed his hand over hers, but it didn't feel the same. It was like a ghost hand, or a chill breeze touching her fingers for a second before moving away.

They pulled out of the small car park and followed the exit road, joining the motorway about a half a mile further along from the point where they'd left it.

The child was already asleep as they crossed over into the fast lane to overtake a large truck. The woman turned her head and looked into the truck's cab. There was a light on in there; it seemed to fill the entire space, a pulsing entity. The truck driver's face was soft and kind. He had a short, neat beard and small blue eyes. He was singing along to a song on the radio. She stared at his mouth, trying to lip read the lyrics—she wished that she knew the name of the tune. It seemed important somehow; the answer to a riddle that might just change everything.

When the truck driver realised that he was being watched, she turned her face away from his gaze. She could feel him staring at her through two layers of glass as they pulled ahead of the truck and drifted back into the slow lane. He flashed his lights, but the man either didn't notice or chose to ignore the gesture.

Her hand was still resting on the man's wide thigh. He was too hot for comfort. She took away her hand and pushed it between her knees. She was cold. She was always cold. She wondered if it was warm inside the cab of that truck.

They drove on into the sodium-spattered darkness with no destination in mind. Traffic was light. The stars were silver pinpricks in the black night sky. Wherever they went, the man encountered monsters, and he tried his best to wipe them out. It was what he did, what he was compelled to do. He knew of no other way to put out the fire that raged in his veins, the flame that burned him up inside.

One question had always haunted her: *What if it's true?*

What if they really were monsters?

She looked down at her lap, at her hand gripped between her knees.

I am not my husband's keeper. I'll never be able to change him.

The thought rattled around inside her head, becoming less than an echo of a truth she'd always avoided.

The woman realised that eventually she'd have to stop him rather than going along with his moods and trying to curb his violent outbursts—even if these poorly stage-managed incidents were all that stopped him from losing his mind completely and hurting her and the child, she knew that she was wrong to allow it.

One day she would have to put an end to this. She would have to, because if she failed to do so then she must surely be as insane as him.

When that day came, she just hoped that she could shield the child from any further harm. She loved the man, but she thought that she loved the child more. And on nights like this one, when the man's blood was boiling, she felt certain of the task ahead of her.

She glanced over at the man.

He was looking directly into her face, as if he was able to read her thoughts. He wasn't smiling. His hands gripped the steering wheel so hard that his knuckles had turned white.

"What were you looking at back there?" His voice was steady and even.

A gun, she thought. *I'll need a gun.*

"Nothing," she said. "I was just staring into space." She braced herself for a slap but it didn't come.

"That man in the truck...I think he was one of them. I think he was a monster." His voice was a whisper.

She didn't say a word. *Where can I get a gun?*

In the back seat, the child stirred, ready to wake. She yawned loudly.

Lights flared in the rear window; the truck she'd seen earlier was approaching at speed. When it overtook them and shifted back over into their lane just ahead of them, a strange smile crossed the man's face. He put his foot down to keep up with the truck, as if he were chasing it. His features had hardened, a likeness carved in stone.

She wondered if this would ever end, or if it would be her life forever.

The road stretched ahead of them, as if in reply to her question. They were racing towards another bright dawn and following a trail of monsters.

Maybe tomorrow, she thought, not for the first time and certainly not for the last. *Maybe tomorrow I'll stop him.*

Up ahead, the brake lights on the truck turned red.

Beside her, the man pulled the knife he'd taken from the tray in the restaurant out of his pocket.

She closed her eyes and tried to think of nothing.

WHAT WE MEAN WHEN WE TALK ABOUT THE DEAD

THE HOUSE LOOKED THE SAME. Nothing had changed since the last time Liz had visited. That was a month ago, when the youngest of the Everley children had been sent home from school with unexplained marks on her arms, which had been noticed by a teacher during a P.E. lesson. There had been no further evidence of abuse on that occasion, but because of the family's past history and their open case file still under review at Social Services, the incident was taken seriously, and another home visit and interview had been more than justified.

Everyone was relieved when it turned out to be a false alarm—the kid had hurt herself on a damaged piece of fencing while she was playing in the garden. The fence was repaired. The parents received a lecture about maintaining their property. She went home to a strong drink and a night in front of the television.

This time, Liz knew, things might not be so simple.

She sat in her car and stared at the stone walls of the old building. It was huge—so much bigger than her own place. Spread over three floors, the Victorian-era terraced house was probably worth a hell of a lot more now than it was when the Everleys had bought it thirty years ago. It had been smaller then, too. Trevor Everley (a name that had always secretly amused her) was a builder, and he had extended the ground floor into the back garden to create more space to accommodate his ever-expanding clan.

It could have been a nice house, number twenty-five Wheatfield Drive, but there was something about the place that kept it from being welcoming. The external walls were dull and weather-worn, the windows were old and their frames rotten, the front door had suffered a lot of abuse and a couple of the glass panels had been removed and replaced with untreated plywood sheets.

The house looked...foreboding. Maybe because of the reasons Liz had been called out here in the past, she always associated this particular house with trouble.

She turned off the engine, got out of her battered old Ford Fiesta, and walked to the front gate. Pausing for a moment, she gathered her thoughts, and then opened the gate and stepped lightly along the path to the door. She knocked three times—an old habit she'd picked up from her father—and waited.

The door was opened by Norma Everley, the mother. "Hello, Liz." She smiled. It wasn't an expression that looked good on her pinched face. Her teeth were bad, yellowing from exposure to tobacco, and her lips were much too thin. She had her hair pulled back into a tight ponytail, was not wearing any makeup (which was unusual for Norma Everley, who normally wouldn't even go to the corner newsagent without her "face" on), and there were dark hollows beneath her dull brown eyes.

"This had better be good, Norma. I had a DVD and a Chinese takeaway planned for this evening, so...well, this had better be worth my time."

Norma opened the door wide and took a few backward steps along the wide hallway. "Come in. We can't talk out there on the doorstep. I don't want everyone knowing my friggin' business, do I?"

Liz stepped inside and closed the door behind her. The house was dark; the bulbs never seemed to shed much light and the windows were always grimy. But Victorian houses were always dark—she knew that. It was nothing to do with the darkness that lay at the heart of this family.

"Is it Trevor? Has he been drinking again?" She took off her coat and hung it on the wooden newel post at the bottom of the stairs. She glanced up the stairwell and saw the youngest child—Skye, the one who had fallen against the garden fence—standing up there clutching a teddy bear. The child smiled, possibly recognising Liz from before. Then Skye turned around and scampered up onto the next floor.

"No. Trevor's been sober for six weeks."

"One of the kids, then? Is Jessica in trouble again? Has she been seeing that boy, the one who sells drugs?"

Norma shook her head. "No...it's nothing like that. None of the usual stuff."

"Listen, Norma, you've only just got your kids back out of foster care, so don't make me take them away again. Next time it'll be for good. You know that, don't you?"

Norma dug a hand-rolled cigarette out of the pocket of her loose-fitting cardigan, lit it with a cheap lighter, and took a long, hard drag. "Fuckin' social workers. You always assume I've been hurting my kids. I love my babies. All of 'em. You know that." She shook her head. Stray hairs came loose from the ponytail, hung down like rats' tails across her forehead.

"Just tell me why you called me. Tell me what's going on so I can try to help and then go home. I'm tired. It's been a long week. The last thing I need is to get caught up in your problems again. I'm sorry, but I explained all this the last time. I'm no longer your case worker. Your file has been passed along the line to someone else."

Norma nodded. Then she pursed her lips. "You're the only one I trust." She blinked, and her eyes were so distant and watery; then they snapped into focus as she stared at Liz's face. There was a strange look in those eyes. Liz thought it looked like pleading.

"Tell me what the problem is, Norma. I'll do my best." She smiled, feeling empty inside. She had her own problems, she didn't need this. Her father was just a week in his grave, her mother was still on medication, and her brother was halfway across the world, building a new life that he kept separate from the rest of them, as if he were trying to hide.

"Come through." Norma turned her back and went into the kitchen. The lights in there were brighter. The shiny surfaces reflected their glow, doubling the illuminative quality. The white goods and appliances were modern, at odds with the shabbiness of the rest of the house. It was as if the Everleys had started to modernize the place and ran out of funds after completing just this one room.

Norma flicked on the kettle and sat down at the breakfast bar. Liz pulled up a stool and followed suit. She stared at the window. The day was draining out of the sky like blood from an open wound.

"Remember when Trevor's dad died, eighteen months ago?"

Liz twitched. Norma's voice had pulled her out of some kind of fugue. "Yes. Yes, I do. I recall that Trevor hit the booze pretty hard after that. He had problems dealing with his emotions towards his father, struggled to get them straight. But he got there in the end."

"Yes." Norma sucked on her cigarette, and then stubbed it out on a small white tea plate. "It was a bad time for us all. But you helped us through. That's why I called you...you were the only one who ever really helped us. All the others—the police, your mates in Social Services—all they wanted to do was stick us with the label of a 'problem family.' That's all they saw when they looked at us: one big problem after another." She paused, rubbed the back of her neck with her right hand. The left one remained on the table, unmoving. "But you saw us differently. You took the time to get to know us, treat us like real people. If it wasn't for you...well, things would have been a lot worse."

Liz glanced down at the table, at her hand. The finger where she'd removed her wedding band had a faint tan line, even now, a year after the divorce had become final. "Just tell me what it is, would you? I'm exhausted. Tomorrow is Saturday, it's my day off. Tell me and we'll try to sort it out." She looked back up. Norma was staring at her, hard; the woman's eyes were as cold as glaciers.

"Trevor's dad's come back."

There was a silence, then, broken only by the slowly rising note of the kettle as the water began to boil. Neither of them spoke for a few seconds. There didn't seem to be much they could say. Norma's statement hung in the air, almost halting further discussion.

"What are you talking about?" Liz felt like standing up and leaving and never coming back here, to this large house and its depthless dark.

"Just that. He's come back. He died eighteen months ago and now he's come back." The kettle made a loud popping sound. The water had boiled, the button flicking outwards.

"You mean he's haunting you? A ghost?" Liz's hand made a fist on the table. She stared at it, became convinced that the hand belonged to someone else, not her. She couldn't even feel her fingers as they curled into her palm. "Come on, Norma. Stop taking the piss. You called me all the way— "

"No, not a ghost!" Norma had raised her voice. She was afraid.

Liz swallowed. "What about that tea, eh?"

Norma got up and walked across to the kettle. She took two mugs from the draining board by the sink and placed a teabag into each. Then she poured over the hot water. "Still take it black, with two sugars?"

"Yes, please."

Norma stirred the teas. She stirred them for ages, taking far too long, stalling for time, trying to keep Liz here.

"Thanks," said Liz as the other woman set down a mug on the table. She remained standing, clutching her tea and staring at a point on the wall that didn't look any different from the rest of the walls: just a flat white rectangle.

Norma sipped her tea. Winced. Blew across the rim of the cup. "He came back last night. When I went upstairs to the attic rooms, to put away some towels, he was there, in his old room, sitting on the edge of the bed with his head in his hands. I thought he was a ghost at first, but then he took away his hands and looked at me. He'd been crying."

Liz was cold. The heating was on, but all she felt was the chill that she'd brought inside with her. Or had it been in here all along, waiting? "This is nonsense," she said. "Utter nonsense."

"Just wait a minute, and ask yourself this one question," said Norma, sitting down again. "Have I ever lied to you? All the time you've known me, the visits you've made to this house...did I ever once lie to you?"

The answer, of course, was no. Trevor had lied about his drinking and his temper. The kids had lied about the times when Trevor had hit them. But Norma...she had never done anything but tell the truth. She had been the one to open up about the intimate details regarding Trevor's violent outbursts; she'd shown her own bruises first, before revealing those on the children. Not once had she ever deceived Liz, not about any of it. However painful, however personal things got, she had never lied.

"Okay," said Liz. "No, you haven't ever lied to me. You've always been honest. That's why I was able to get you your kids back, and why they're still here now."

"They're sleeping over at a friend's house, before you ask. All of them except the youngest—she's asleep in her room. They don't know about any of this. It would terrify them. I wouldn't even know how to tell them."

Liz let out a breath. It was louder than she expected. "You can't expect me to believe any of this. Come on, woman, don't be so damn silly. This can only get you into trouble again. Tell me the real reason you begged me to come out here. Has Trevor been violent again? Is he hitting you or the kids?"

"He's upstairs now."

"Who, Trevor?"

"No, his dad. Trevor's at work. He works nights now, at the factory. He left me here...all alone, with *him*. He couldn't deal with any of this." She raised her eyes towards the ceiling. Then, slowly, she lifted her mug and took another drink.

"Norma..." But Liz didn't know what to say.

"I'll take you up there, but I won't go in. I'll stay outside, on the landing. You can go in there and talk to him. He does talk. He talks, but his voice doesn't sound the same. It's all dry and raspy-like."

Liz stood, slamming down her cup onto the breakfast bar. The sound was like a gunshot in the small kitchen. "Okay. I'll go up there. Then, when I find that room empty, I want to know the real reason why I'm here. Got that?"

Norma nodded. She looked away: at the sink, at the window, at the pots and pans on the draining board. Anywhere but directly into Liz's eyes.

They climbed the stairs in silence. Liz followed Norma up the narrow staircase, turned right onto the first-floor landing, and then took the final set of stairs on her own.

"I can't go back up there. I'm sorry." Norma looked down at her shoes. She shook her head. "I'm sorry."

Liz grasped the handrail and slowly began to ascend. The old stairs creaked; the handrail was loose, coming away slightly from the wall. When she reached the topmost landing, she turned to face the room she remembered as belonging to Trevor's father. She couldn't remember the old man's name, but she recalled his face. It was a hard face, the face of a working man who'd spent his entire life fighting to find his place in the world. He was not a nice man, Mr. Everley senior, and Liz had never warmed to him. She'd been relieved when he died. His absence in the house had seemed to lift a weight that Trevor had always carried, allowing him to look at himself and accept his own failings: the frailty of his ego, his reliance on anger as the only method by which he could ever demonstrate his feelings.

Liz reached out and gripped the door handle. She turned it slowly, feeling trepidation hold her back as she pushed open the door. A streak of weak light bloomed faintly in the gap between door and frame. She opened the door and stepped into the room, turning left as she did so to face the bed that was pushed up against the wall that ran along the middle of the house.

She noticed the smell first: a light aroma of lilies and dust.

He was sitting on the bed staring at the wardrobe. He was wearing the suit in which he had been buried, his hair was neatly combed, and his hands rested motionless in his lap, the fingers knotted together like a puzzle made of flesh and bone.

There was a strange sense of stillness in the room that did not feel natural, as if everything had been posed deliberately before she walked in, and set up that way to create a specific effect. The lamp on the bedside drawers looked like a prop from a film.

This was the same man who had died. She knew it was true; there could be no mistake. He had the same tough face, tight lips, and bushy grey eyebrows; the same short, wide legs, large hands, and pigeon chest. It was him. It was the dead man. Just as Norma had said, he had come back to the family home.

"Hello," she said, unable to move further into the room.

He did not move. He just kept staring at the wardrobe. The side of his face was pale. His eyes were wide open.

"My name is Liz Balfour...we met a few times before. We met when..." *Back when you were alive.*

Suddenly she had the urge to laugh. The whole situation was ludicrous, like something out of a comedy show. None of this, she tried to convince herself, could possibly be real. It was a trick, a bad joke somebody was playing on her.

"Do you remember me, Mr. Everley?"

"Yes." His voice was grating, as if he were speaking through a mouthful of gravel. He turned his head and looked at her. His hands stayed where they were, in his lap, and his torso did not budge. His head simply swivelled on his neck, the skin of his throat bunching up because it was so loose, like a scarf.

Liz was not afraid. She knew that she should be, and that she had every right to run screaming from the room. But this wasn't that kind of situation. She didn't feel as if she was in danger of any kind, and the old man did nothing but sit on the bed, staring at her. He wasn't scary. He was sad.

"Do you know where you are?" She took a tiny step forward—so small that it was barely even a proper step. She just moved her toes forward an inch across the carpet.

"Yes," he said again, but this time something dribbled from between his lips and spilled down the front of his suit jacket. It was dirt. There was soil coming out of his mouth.

You're dead, she thought. *You're really fucking dead.*

"Can you say anything more than that? Can you speak...properly?"

He nodded. "I can speak. I have words. They feel strange in my mouth, like they aren't my own, but I have them." That voice: it was terrible, like his teeth had been smashed in and he was speaking through the debris.

"Do you know where you've been?"

"I've been dead."

She tried to swallow, but her mouth was too dry. She flexed her fingers, curled her toes inside her sensible shoes, trying to root herself in reality. "You were dead?"

He nodded again. "Yes. Dead."

"But you aren't now?"

"Yes."

"What do you mean, 'yes'? Do you mean that you aren't dead anymore? That you're alive? Is that it? They buried you alive?" She was grasping for a reason, an explanation, however unlikely.

"No. I mean that I'm still dead. I'm dead but I've come back home."

Liz wanted badly to sit down, but there were no chairs in the room. It had been cleared after his death, leaving only the wardrobe, a set of drawers, and the single bed upon which he was sitting, his dead face turned towards her, his dead eyes taking her in.

"Why have you come back here?"

"I don't know." His face was devoid of expression. He'd either forgotten how to move his features or was unable to, she wasn't sure which. It was like talking to a mechanical toy, or a shop window mannequin with a voice box fitted inside its chest. There was very little about the man that seemed human.

"What can you remember about where you've been?"

She thought of her own father, lying in a fresh hole in the ground these past seven days, and she realized why she was not afraid. Because if this was really happening—if this man had actually returned from the grave—then wasn't it possible that her own father might do just the same? Might not he in fact be at home now, waiting for her in a dim room, with his hands in his lap and a mouth full of grave dirt?

He tilted his head to one side, like a dog trying to communicate with its master. "I remember...I remember the dark. The cold, tight, unbearable dark. It hurt. There was no air. I couldn't breathe. Then I didn't need to breathe. Everything stopped. Then I woke up. I remember the sounds of small animals and insects digging through the soil, and distant singing, like a choir." He stopped speaking and closed his eyes. She heard the clicking of his eyelids.

"How did you get out? Did somebody help you?"

His eyes remained closed. "I don't know. The next thing I remember is being here, on this bed. My bed. I was sitting with my head in my hands, trying to cry. Then my daughter-in-law came into the room and she screamed." He opened his eyes. "She screamed and she ran back out, and there was nothing I could do to help her."

Liz reached out and grabbed the wall to steady herself. The whole room was rocking back and forth, as if she were standing on the deck of a ship. The ocean was rough; the seas were treacherous. She was afraid she might fall in and drown.

"She came back in and she combed my hair. She was crying." He paused, but did not take a breath. There was no need: he was dead. "They don't want me here, do they?"

There was such an ache of sadness in his voice that Liz felt her eyes begin to swim. Tears rolled down her cheeks, hot against her skin.

"They want me to go away, to go back. But I can't. I have nowhere else to go."

Liz was shaking her head. "I don't know. Really, I have no idea."

"But I can't go back. I don't know how. And I don't know why I'm here, or for how long. None of this makes any sense. I was dead. I still am dead. But I'm here. Why am I here? What happened to make me come back?"

Liz felt her legs buckle, failing beneath the dead weight of her body. She sank to the floor, bending her knees and hitting the carpet with an audible thud. She was cold again. There was a breeze inside the room. The windows were shut, but somehow a stray draught had entered.

"What am I supposed to do?" The old man's quavering, rugged voice was desperate. He was lost.

Liz crawled across the floor to the bed, dragging herself upright using the edge of the duvet. The old man did not make a move to help her, but he watched her every inch of the way. She hauled herself up and sat down next to him on the mattress, taking hold of one of his gnarled old hands, wrapping it up in one of her own much smaller hands, and began to stroke the weathered skin of his fingers.

"*What should I do?*"

Liz stared into the shallows of his eyes, seeing no answers but not seeking them anyway, not here, in this godforsaken place. There were too many questions that could never be answered; there was too much confusion in this world and whatever lay beyond. So she took him in her arms and she held him, pulling him close to her body, his cold, hard, lifeless chest like a slab of concrete as it pressed up against her soft breasts. "I don't know," she said, solemnly, "but I promise you I'll try to find out."

WHAT WE MEAN WHEN WE TALK ABOUT THE DEAD

After a while, she left him there, in the room, and went slowly back outside. Norma was sitting on the stairs, clutching her arms and rocking gently, reciting a prayer under her breath.

"Go to him," said Liz, breathlessly, her voice a savage whisper. "Make him feel welcome, for God's sake." Rage poured through her, almost breaking her in half. Tiny white stars exploded in her view. "Go and make him feel at home, damn it!"

She brushed past the other woman and ran down the stairs, grabbing her coat when she reached the ground floor. She opened the front door, looked back once, and saw the same child she'd noticed before, young Skye, huddled in the shadows just below the landing, clutching her grubby teddy bear by one torn arm.

She smiled; the child smiled back, but shyly, before backing away into darkness.

Wiping the tears from her eyes, Liz turned around and went home to see who might be waiting there for her.

UNICORN MEAT

IT DOESN'T REALLY MATTER WHEN I found the unicorn. I think it had always been in my life, waiting for me to notice it there: a tale waiting to be told, a mystery to be unravelled. Maybe it was hiding in the shadows, or perhaps I wasn't able to see the animal until I reached a certain age, a specific point in my existence.

All I do know is that I found it there, near the old tin shed in the back lane, a few weeks after my twelfth birthday.

The following day I took my sister, Jessie, to see the unicorn. It was just after school. Not quite dark yet. She was excited when I told her that I had a secret, and that she couldn't tell anybody what I was about to show her. In truth, I still wasn't sure if I'd really seen it myself.

"Can Dolly come?" she asked, dragging her battered old Cabbage Patch doll along by one arm. I hated that doll—it was ugly.

"Sure," I said. "I don't see why not."

We went out of the house, through the gap in the fence at the bottom of the back garden, and across the little area of waste ground to the cobbled alley. It was late in the year. The sun was dipping behind the roofs of the old terraced houses at the edge of town and there was a chill in the air. Jessie held onto my hand. Her grip was surprisingly strong for one so young.

"Is it far?" Her voice was tiny.

"Not really. Just a little way along the lane."

We walked past the old asbestos garages and the spot where people always dumped old furniture. I was never sure who the tin shed belonged to, or what was inside, but it was always locked. I assumed it was used by one of the neighbourhood bad boys to store stolen property. It was that kind of area—the kind where black market goods weren't really an issue, and nobody cared where an item came from as long as they could buy it cheap.

"This way," I whispered. I wasn't sure why I was talking so quietly. It just felt right. I didn't want to speak too loudly in case whatever magic dwelled in this place was shattered, like a glass ornament.

The grass at the back of the tin shed was overgrown, knee-height. There were broken bottles, shattered crockery, empty food wrappers, and other varieties of litter scattered around the area. Near the base of the tin wall, there was a long, narrow crack. Its edges were rusty: a dark red tinge, like old bloodstains. The tin had peeled back a little to form a lip. I knelt down in front of the crack and started to speak in a coaxing manner. "Come on, boy," I said. "We won't hurt you." I didn't even know if it was a boy. At that point, I wasn't even sure if it was real. But whatever I had seen before, it had disappeared through this gap.

Jessie remained silent. She seemed to pick up on the atmosphere.

Before long, I heard a shuffling sound. Then, louder, what could only be something moving close to the damaged tin wall but on the other side. There came a small whinnying noise, tiny hooves clopping in the dirt. Then the unicorn appeared, pushing its nose through the crack, which was followed by its neck, its body...

The unicorn was about the size of a small Jack Russell dog. Its legs were short, stunted—different from the long, muscular haunches I'd read about in books of fairy tales. There were scars along its flanks. Its mane was grubby and tatty, a mucky grey colour rather than white. One of its legs was lame; it walked with a slight limp.

The horn at the centre of its forehead wasn't the graceful spiral I'd also read about in books. It was just a thin, tapered appendage; a protruding bone that ended in a tapered point.

"Hello, boy."

The unicorn rubbed the side of its head against my outstretched hand, and then began to nuzzle my palm.

"It's okay."

I could feel its hot breath on my skin. Only then did I admit it was real.

"Good boy."

The unicorn licked my fingers, pushed its nose against my fingertips.

Jessie didn't say a word. I wasn't sure if she was scared or in awe. It was a beautiful sight, after all, no matter how unlikely. A tiny unicorn in a vacant lot behind a rusted tin shed.

After a short while the unicorn retreated back inside the shed. I didn't know if it lived there, or if it simply liked to hide in the darkness. I wondered if anyone else knew of its existence, but then decided that they probably didn't. None of the locals could keep their mouths shut about anything: the news of a dwarf version of some mythical beast living in the tin shed would have spread throughout the populace like a bad debt.

I stood. Jessie grabbed my hand.

"Was it real?"

I couldn't answer her; I was once again unsure. I wasn't certain about much. Not the whereabouts of our mother, or the reliability of our father. Not the future or the past. Not even the present.

I squeezed her hand. "Come on. We'll be late for tea." We walked back along the lane, across the waste ground, and climbed back through the gap in the fence. When I saw our house I felt like running away. Taking her somewhere she would be safe. But I couldn't. There was no other place I could think of to be. This was my home. However much I hated it, I lived here. We both did.

There were no distant lands ruled by benign kings to which we could escape. The wardrobe in our bedroom would not provide access to some enchanted world. The alley led only to an industrial estate, not some enchanted forest.

This was it: home. There was nothing else.

Dad was drunk again. I could smell the liquor on his breath, and he made beans on toast for tea rather than cook something more substantial. That was always the big giveaway: if we ate crap, he was drunk. When he was sober he liked to cook us all a proper meal, pretending to be a real parent rather than the fake one he so obviously was. I'm sure he'd tried hard once, perhaps when Mum was around, but these days it was all he could do to throw some slop on a plate before opening another can of beer in front of the TV.

"Eat up. I'm going to watch my programmes." He slouched towards the fridge, took out a can of ale, opened it, and shuffled through into the lounge.

"Another night in the magic kingdom," I said, quiet enough that he wouldn't hear.

We ate in silence. Even Jessie was quiet.

After we'd eaten—and I'd opened a tin of peaches in pear juice for our pudding—Jessie and I headed for the stairs. As we walked past the open lounge door, I glanced inside and saw Dad sitting there on the ratty sofa, smiling at the TV. I wasn't sure what he was watching—a Western, some sporting highlights, or a game show—but it pleased him. He raised a can to his lips and took a swallow of beer.

"Wait." The sound of his voice was a hammer falling.

I crept back to the open door and looked inside.

He spoke without turning away from the TV, presenting to me only his profile: "Watch what you're doing out there. I know you've been hanging around in the lane. There are some queer types in this town. Some old tramp's been flashing his cock to kids." He drank again from his can. "Stay away from there." He said nothing more; his silence was my order to leave.

"Yes, Dad."

He grunted. I walked away.

Upstairs, Jessie and I played Top Trumps. The Monster pack: my favourite. Jessie preferred the car ones, even though she had no interest in motor vehicles. I think she liked the colours of the different autos.

After a few games she started to get tired. I smiled and put away the cards. "Bedtime."

She nodded, stifling a yawn.

I led her into her room—the box room, the smallest in the house—and didn't insist that she cleaned her teeth first. It was my way of doing her a favour.

"You need the toilet?"

She shook her head and slipped into bed, pulling the covers up under her chin.

"Night, then."

"Night," she said, eyes already closing.

I walked out of the room, switching off the light but leaving the door ajar. Jessie didn't like to sleep in complete darkness in case she woke up and it scared her. She liked to see a sliver of landing light at the edge of the door.

I went to the toilet, didn't bother brushing my teeth either, had a piss and then went back to my room. The curtains were open. I could see the sickle moon above a bank of grey clouds. I stared at the moon for what felt like a long time but was probably only a matter of minutes. I wondered if Mum could see the moon wherever she was.

My limbs felt heavy as soon as I got into bed. My body sagged into the too-soft mattress. A greyness that reminded me of those clouds washed over me, obscuring my vision, weighing down my eyelids with a soft pressure. I'd wanted to read for a little while, but tiredness pushed me under.

I dreamed a lot back then, mostly about my absent mother. But that night I did not dream. Not really. There were visions in my head, painted behind my eyes, but they could not be described as dreams. Motionless pictures, like photographs. Dad, Mum, Jessie and I, smiling and standing on a beach we'd never visited in real life; then again, in the same poses, standing on an empty street somewhere; finally, I saw us loitering beside the tin shed, those same manic smiles frozen onto our faces. I sensed a sort of barely-repressed panic behind the pictures, as if we were fighting back some kind of brute terror, a concentration of dread that might consume the entire world if we let it out.

I woke in the dark. I could make out the shapes of the furniture in my room, but none of it seemed like mine. I felt as if I'd woken in a replica of my bedroom, a room that had been fashioned to look like mine but felt nothing at all like it. There was no trace of me in this place; despite being present, in my bed, I wasn't really here.

Before I could examine this idea fully, I drifted back into a deep sleep. This time there were no pictures; there was just a huge and pitiless blackness into which I slowly fell.

The next day was Saturday so there was no school. Dad stayed in bed late with a hangover, so I made breakfast for Jessie. I wasn't hungry; I drank a glass of milk and watched her eat, feeling sad and cold inside. I wished Mum had stayed. I wished that she hadn't run off like she did. Jessie needed a mother. This house needed her presence so that it might once again become a home.

After breakfast I went outside into the yard. My football was lying against the wall. It was partially deflated; I'd kicked it against something sharp a few days before. I picked it up and squeezed it. There was still some air inside. Sighing, I threw the ball onto the ground and began to dribble it in slow circles, practicing my footwork. I was good at football. I always had been. Back when Dad had allowed me to play for a local team, a scout from one of the big clubs had come to watch me play. When Dad found out, he pulled me from the team. He was like that: any sniff of potential success for anyone and he would do his best to smother it.

After a few minutes I let the ball roll away from me and left the yard. I walked round the streets, not with any destination in mind, just enjoying the movement. The sky was overcast but the sun was doing its best to be seen through the light grey clouds. Somewhere a dog was barking—the noise was toneless and incessant, like a recording stuck on a loop. I started to walk away from the barking sound, and before long I found myself approaching the place Dad had ordered me to stay clear of, but from a different route than usual.

I saw the tramp a long time before he saw me. I probably should have turned around and gone somewhere else—anywhere but here. Or home. Instead I kept walking. Something inside me—some nascent rebellious streak—didn't like the idea of either my father or this scruffy vagrant dictating where I hung out in my free time.

The tramp was sitting with his back against the tin shed. The remains of a fire smoked near his feet. There was a rolled up sleeping bag and a plastic carrier bag filled with what looked like rags lying next to him. He looked up, smiled. His hair was long beneath the floppy hat he wore; his eyes were dull and narrow; his thin mouth was surrounded by straggly facial hair.

"Hello there, son." He smiled. Most of his teeth were missing.

I ignored him—or pretended to.

"Wanna see something interesting?"

I thought about the small unicorn, its damaged leg, how its horn flashed in the sunlight. I didn't realise what I was doing, and by the time I registered that I'd stopped walking it was too late.

"Yeah, thought so. Everyone wants to see something interesting, eh? Hard to resist..." He rose slowly to his feet, leaning against the side of the tin shed. He looked so old and slow that I knew I could outrun him if I had to, but still I shuffled back a few steps, maintaining a good distance between us.

"No need to be scared," said the tramp. He smiled again; a knife wound in his face. "I ain't gonna hurt you. Not me. I'm too old and too tired for that."

He started to fumble with the front of his pants, and before my brain had the chance to catch up with what my eyes were seeing, he had his dick in his hands. It was small, fat, and hard.

"Come on, lad. Give it a wee stroke, eh? Just stroke my little pet..." He started to shuffle forward, moving towards me, and then the shuffle became a run. He'd been faking; he could move easily, and swiftly.

I turned around and burst into a sprint. Behind me, I could hear his phlegm-addled breath. I moved my legs faster, and then, unable to resist, I threw a glance over my shoulder.

The tramp had stopped chasing me. He was standing with his back to me, in a shallow crouch, one arm held out in front of him. "Hey, now...what the hell are you?"

Moving to one side for a better view, I looked beyond the filthy old man. There, standing in the dirt beside the dying embers of the tramp's fire, was the unicorn. *My* unicorn.

"Come on, then...come and see what I got for you." The tramp shuffled forward, inching towards the unbelievable creature.

The unicorn cocked its head to one side, lifted one of its front hooves—the left one, I think—and stamped lightly, three times, on the ground. It raised its head and flared its nostrils.

"No," I whispered. "No!" The second time I think I actually screamed the word.

The tramp looked back at me, grinning. "You stroke me or I'll stroke your pet. I'll stroke it hard." His eyes were flat and dead, just like old pennies.

Then, thankfully, the unicorn turned away and scampered clumsily into the long weeds behind the tin shed. I'm still not sure what spooked it—the inherent threat of the tramp, something in my posture, or perhaps it was some instinct of its own that told the animal things were not good.

"Little bastard," said the tramp. I wasn't sure if he meant me or the unicorn.

I ran. I did not stop running until I was home, and the only thing that made me stop running was the thought of Jessie in there with Dad. If it weren't for her, I think I would have run harder and faster and further a long time before that day.

"Where've you been?" Dad's words were slurred. He seemed to be drunk earlier in the day lately, as if this was the only thing that could get him through. Weekends were the worst because he didn't have to remain sober for work. During the week, he only drank at night; on Saturdays and Sundays he pretty much started on the sauce when he got out of bed and didn't quit until he passed out on the sofa in the evening.

"Nowhere, Dad. Just out...walking around..."

My answer seemed to satisfy him. He went into the kitchen,

opened the fridge, and took out another beer. He sat down at the dining table. I couldn't hear a thing. I couldn't even hear him breathing. I stood there, outside the kitchen door, for what seemed like ages before the clicking of glass brought me fully back into the moment.

Jessie was upstairs. I went into her room and played with her for a while, then read to her from one of her books—something about a cat on an adventure around the world in a hot air balloon. She loved stories about people running away. Perhaps it made her feel better about Mum's absence.

"Can I see it again?"

Her question took me by surprise. I'd paused in my reading, thinking she might have fallen asleep because she was curled up with Dolly on the bed.

"What's that, Jess?"

"The little horsey...the horsey with the horn."

I nodded. "Maybe tomorrow."

"I wanna see it today. I wanna pick it up and give it a cuddle."

She always wanted to do that, hold everything too close. Cats gave her a wide berth; dogs seemed to sense that she wanted to manhandle them and tensed at her approach. She had so much love to give, and only me to accept it. But I wasn't enough; I was never enough. She needed more. Like a bucket overflowing with too much water, her love was slopping over the sides and staining the ground, wasted.

"Not now, baby." I stroked her hair and held back tears, the source of which I didn't understand. I climbed onto the bed alongside her and held her tight, still holding back those tears. I didn't want to let them go; they felt valuable somehow, perhaps even sacred.

I'm not sure who went to asleep first, me or Jessie, but when I opened my eyes again she was gone. I looked out the window. The sky was darker, but it was not yet night.

I went downstairs. Dad was in the living room, flaked out in front of the television. Empty bottles surrounded him like silent spectators; in his hand, he was throttling one of their brethren. His eyes were locked onto the screen, but he didn't see a thing.

I stood in the hallway and felt cold and alone. I'd never felt so abandoned in my life. No mother, no father, and my little sister slipping away from me more and more with each day that passed. I walked softly into the kitchen; the back door was ajar. She'd gone outside, and I could make an educated guess to where she might be headed.

I put on my jacket and went outside. It was colder than it had been earlier that day. The sun had slid away, giving up the good fight. The clouds were thicker and darker, like a hoard of bad things waiting to happen.

I drifted through the gap in the back fence, glided across the patch of waste ground, and set foot upon the cobbles of the alley. The tin shed seemed to glow in the fading light; it was like a beacon, or a warning pyre.

Jessie was standing in the alley, her hands behind her back and her weight on one leg. The tramp was seated, smiling up at her. His slits of eyes were focused only on my sister; he didn't even see me coming.

The fire had burned out a little while ago but the embers still glowed faintly, as if from a distance—light from another world. He'd assembled a makeshift spit from some twigs and tied them together with coils of old, rusted wire. Even as I approached, I could make out what he had been roasting there, on the fire...

Its ribcage had been split open, and a stick rammed into its mouth to penetrate its body and emerge through its hindquarters. The horn was burned but still intact, sticking out from its charred little head. The meat had been stripped from its flanks and belly; the burned bones of its vertebrae were perfectly visible along its crooked back, where the meat there had been cut away. It could not have made for a very large meal, but I suspected the tramp had eaten poorer fare in his time.

In that moment, everything focused to a point of clarity: my mother was never coming back; my father would sink deeper into alcoholism and the casual backhanders, the occasional playful yet slightly-too-hard kidney punches, would soon transform into more overt forms of abuse; my sister would become as much a victim as I was, and some day her life would cease to hold even the smallest hint of potential.

Everything positive would be ground down, worn away. The unicorn meat on the spit would be consumed; the slivers of hope we still clung to would go the same way, sucked into the maw of something rancid.

The tears I'd been holding back earlier—the ones I'd held in check for so long—spilled out onto my cheeks. They seared my flesh like acid.

As I got closer, I could hear what Jessie was saying. "I don't want to. It isn't nice."

The tramp's hands strayed to his lap but his eyes never left her face. "Just a little stroke," he said. "Then you can help me finish off this nice dinner." He nodded towards the smoking embers and the scraps of meat still hanging from the jerry-built spit.

I'm not sure quite when I picked up the metal bar, but there were countless similar objects lying around out there and I could have taken my pick. It felt good in my hand, an extension of my body rather than something external. For a second, the metal bar felt both unbelievably light and depressingly heavy at the same time. It made my bones ache in a way that was not unpleasant.

Jessie was shaking her head. She looked to be on the verge of tears.

I remembered something my mother had once told me, a long time ago, once upon a time in a land that now seemed like something out of a fairy tale. She had never been one for giving advice, so what little she did offer tended to stick.

"Never let anyone kill your dreams," she'd said. I always imagined her mouthing those words in a low voice, as she rocked me to sleep. "And if anyone tries, you do the same to them. Be quick and hard and act without pity."

Tears streaked down my face. The clouds above us seemed to shiver.

"Go home, Jessie." My voice sounded different, older; the voice of a man, not a child.

The tramp's eyes locked onto mine, and I think in that moment he knew. He knew that all stories had to have an ending and his was close at hand.

"It came back," he said, shrugging. "I was hungry."

He acted as if that explained everything...

There were no more words. He simply closed his mean little eyes and waited for what was about to happen. His lips moved as he chewed the remains of his last meal. I could see grease in the coarse, matted hair of his beard. This final detail was the one that hurt most of all.

The blood rushed in my ears, a storm approaching.

Jessie moved away, ran back along the alley. I could hear her shoes clattering on the cobbles, making a sound like firecrackers. I didn't have much time. When she got home, Dad would come to see what had upset her so much and take even this small victory away from me.

The truth filled me, flowing with the blood through my veins. Fairy tales were not real. There was no mystery in my world, no magic.

Only this: a moment of beautiful violence, heralded by a glorious aching of the bones, the sight of a shrunken, fire-blackened unicorn horn, the sound of distant thunder in my ears.

I clenched my fingers tighter around the metal bar and bore down upon the waiting tramp. If I heeded my mother's words—was fast enough and hard enough and pitiless enough—he would barely even know what hit him.

CINDER IMAGES

FADE IN: BEETHOVEN'S *PASTORAL SYMPHONY* Number 6, slow and sweet. No title bar or opening credits.

It starts with a little girl, running.

She is young—perhaps eight or nine years old—and she is pumping her arms and her legs as she runs along a dirt road. Behind her, fire burns a line along the horizon. Around her, there is scorched and blackened earth and the burnt-out ruins of redbrick buildings. The girl is partially naked; her upper body is bare, her lower body is clad in torn rags. Her face is dirty, her cheeks are burnt. Flaps of ruined skin hang off her arms and legs, revealing pale pink patches beneath.

This could be Vietnam, it could be Cambodia; it might be Serbia, Afghanistan, or the West Bank. It could be anywhere, at any time.

But it is England.

It is now.

The girl keeps on running even though the soles of her feet are worn away and bleeding. She feels no pain; she is beyond simple feelings. Her mother and father are dead. Her brothers and sisters have been blown apart by the bombs and bullets of an unknown enemy.

A single gunshot rings out and a bullet takes her down. The hair at the right side of her head puffs out; blood and brain and bone spatter in a vivid arc, spraying the grey ground red.

She falls, limp.

Dead.

The audience leans forward, trying to catch the girl; or are they just desperate to get a better view, a closer look at the blood and the carnage?

The music on the soundtrack soars, triumphant.

You try to close your eyes but you cannot. You have to see—you *need* to see this. There are things that must be endured, sights that cannot be ignored. You owe it to the girl; her lonely death must not go unwitnessed. So you sit there with your eyes forced open, taking it all in.

The screen goes dark. The lights come up.

"And that, ladies and gentlemen," says a low, cultured voice through a hidden speaker, "is our little war project."

A ripple of polite applause.

You grit your teeth.

When you glance down at your hands, you see that you are clapping too, but you don't know why, or for whom the applause is intended. The lights turn red and it looks like blood on your hands. You start to rub them together, but the stains remain.

When the lights flicker a signal for the end of the performance and the rest of the audience members start to leave, you pick up your bag from underneath your seat, stand, and walk out with them. You feel numb. Your skin is cold.

Out in the foyer, a fat man in a black suit and John Lennon spectacles is shaking people's hands, answering questions, and posing to have his photograph taken. He is the director, the creative mind behind the brief decontextualised images you have just seen.

"Thank you, thank you," he says, soaking up the kudos, filling up with misplaced pride.

"When will the finished film be available to screen in full?" A local reporter jabs a digital tape recorder into the director's fat face.

"Soon," says the director. "Very soon."

"What will it be called?"

The director opens his arms, lifts his head. "*Cinder Images*," he says in a loud voice, making sure that everyone can hear. His eyes are bright behind the lenses of his glasses.

You consider approaching him to ask why you were invited to the screening, but then think better of such a rash move. It might draw attention to your discomfort. They might stare at you and see the fear that lies beneath your shell.

So you walk outside, into the cold night air, and try to breathe again. The glassed-in posters on the multiplex walls advertise action movies, romantic comedies, films about comic book superheroes. There is no mention of the teaser footage you have just seen; this was a private show, for members of the press and a few lucky winners of competitions. You got hold of your ticket at the underground station, when a publicity man in a fake hazmat suit pushed it into your hand, smiling and nodding his pale, bald head.

"Free show," he'd whispered, as if it were a secret. "Just for you. It must be your lucky day."

Curiosity brought you here, and disgust sends you away. It was not your kind of film. Those images were not something you like to see. Or were they? The film has summoned questions about yourself that you'd rather not answer, not right now.

"How was the movie?"

You turn to see a woman leaning against the boot of a red car. She is smoking a cigarette. Her tiny hands move quickly through the air; her face is delicate, like that of an exquisite china doll.

"Excuse me?" You stop walking but wish you hadn't. You should have just carried on out of the car park.

"The film. Any good? I tried to get in, but they wouldn't let me. I didn't have a ticket."

"If I'd have known, you could have had mine."

"That bad, eh?" She blows out smoke. It hangs in a small white cloud before her small dark eyes.

"Just...disturbing."

"Yes, he's known for that—the director. It's his speciality."

You shrug and begin to move away, unable to think of anything else to say.

"Hang on a minute." She stubs out her cigarette on the car bumper and follows you. Her long, dark coat hangs open to reveal a tight-fitting midnight-blue blouse; she has on either leggings or skin-tight jeans, and a pair of ankle boots with long, spiked heels. She looks alternative; not your type at all.

"It's dark," she says, as if that explains everything. "I'm cold."

Somehow you end up going for a drink in a pub near the cinema. It's busy but not packed; the customers all seem in good cheer. You order a pint of beer for yourself and vodka for the woman. She hasn't told you her name and you don't feel much like asking. She's attractive, but you sense trouble. Maybe even outright danger.

"Thanks," she says, accepting the drink. She takes off her coat and grabs a table just as a group of people get up to leave. Once you are both seated, she undoes the top two buttons of her blouse. The skin on her breastbone is red, livid. Her fingernails are painted black.

"Cheers," you say, lifting your glass to your mouth.

She smiles. Takes a tiny sip of vodka and brushes her foot against your leg under the table. Just when you convince yourself that it was accidental, she does it again.

You feel your cheeks go hot. You start to blink uncontrollably.

"Don't be shy," she says. "I do this all the time."

You have no idea what she means. Or you do and you are unwilling to admit it.

Several drinks later and you're both sitting in the back of a taxi heading out of town, to her place. She licks the side of your neck and her hand strays into your lap. This is not the kind of thing that ever happens to you—you're either lucky or have walked head-first into some kind of disaster. Only time will tell.

She lives in a ground-floor flat opposite a row of shops and an Italian restaurant. The restaurant is empty; most of the shops are boarded up. You have no idea where you are. The streets are unfamiliar and you were too caught up in the moment to look out the window and follow the route.

The skin on the side of your neck is still damp from her tongue.

She grabs your hand and pulls you out of the car. She waits at the kerb while you pay the fare. The taxi driver doesn't even look up at you as he accepts the money. Then he drives away without thanking you for the tip.

Upstairs, her flat is like a showroom: minimal furniture, zero clutter, no photos, no pictures on the white walls. There's not even a stereo or a television to keep her company.

"I live alone," she whispers. "I don't like to keep a lot of stuff around me."

She pours two glasses of whisky without asking and smiles as you swallow yours in one mouthful. She tops up the glasses and smiles again. There's something different about her; on her own turf, she seems less aggressive, more passive.

"I don't usually do this...it's not my style."

"Don't worry," she says. "I've had a lot of practice." She slips off her blouse and takes off her bra. Then she unpeels the leggings and stands there in just her panties, sipping her drink and watching you, waiting to see what you will do.

She has a lot of tattoos. Thin black lines curl around her upper arms, purple flowers erupt on her stomach, and a thick dragon is wrapped around her right thigh.

"You're beautiful." Your voice sounds strange, as if it's a struggle to speak.

"I know," she says. "That's why I got the role."

She turns away and walks lightly across the carpet. You stare at the stylised tattoos of thick black medical stitches down her spine, her tight little backside, the back of her well-toned legs. You finish your second whisky and start to feel drunk. Not just on the alcohol—but on the situation, too. Years ago, you might have dreamed of this moment, but now that it's actually happening you are unsure of how to act.

She opens a door, stops, glances over her bare shoulder. Her smile is as wide as the heavens. It's obvious what she wants you to do.

You wait until the door closes behind her before following her across the room. You don't want to seem too keen, in case she changes her mind. The thought makes you smile; the fear drops away.

You approach the door and stop, reaching out to touch the handle. You play your fingers across the brass knob, teasing yourself with the proximity of her body on the other side. Then, feeling silly, you turn the handle and open the door.

When you enter the room she is face down on the bed. She is naked. Her panties are balled up on the floor at the foot of the bed. She is lying on her stomach, with her backside raised up in the air. She turns her head and stares at you. Her eyes are dark; her skin is pale; her teeth are bright.

"Why me?" You've wanted to ask the question since she first

approached you.

"Why not?" she says, and gives you one of her self-satisfied smiles.

You move slowly across the room and stand at the side of the bed, realising that you should be taking off your clothes and climbing onto the mattress beside her. But something is holding you back—images from the film clip you saw earlier are stirring inside your head.

"That's right," she says. "Just let it come." Her legs tremble. She clenches her fists and raises her arms above her head, grabbing the headboard. The muscles in her forearms tense, becoming rigid. She is preparing for something.

You realise that there is somebody else in the room with you. When you turn your head to the side, you see the little girl from the film. She is crouching down in the corner of the room, large flaps of skin hanging like a ruined flag around her shoulders, and she's covering her face with her battered hands. She is crying but there is no sound.

"Shall I turn it up?" The woman on the bed sits up and turns around. She grabs a remote-control handset from a cabinet at the side of the bed and points it at the girl. The sound leaks gradually into the room, the volume rising steadily. The girl's sobs are heartbreaking, and underscored with a soft classical music score. You wonder if she knows that you are there, and that you can hear her weeping.

You can do nothing but stand and stare, and after a short while it becomes uncomfortable. You experience the same feelings of shame and sadness as you did while watching the film, but this time the emotions are real. They have context.

"What is this?" You take a step forward and then stop, unable to continue. "What's happening here?"

"This is the footage you never got to see." Her voice is like a song; it holds a tune, but one you can barely recognise. "This is what happens when the cameras are turned off and the film crew go home.

This is what's left behind, the outtakes."

The girl is still crying. Her shoulders are hitching up and down; she is pulling at her hair with her small, dirty hands. She lowers her arms and looks up, staring right at you, right through you.

Where her eyes should be there are only burnt and blackened holes, the edges crisped. Deep inside the holes that take up most of the upper part of her face, you can see flickering yellow flames. There's a fire inside the girl, but you aren't sure if it's one that was started by the things she has seen or if it was already there, smouldering quietly.

"What did you think this was—a seduction?" The woman on the bed begins to laugh. The girl joins in, and when she opens her mouth there are no teeth in her gums. Flames curl out of her mouth, between her lips and down across her chin. Her cheeks bulge outwards, the skin turning red and almost transparent.

The woman stands up and walks away from the bed. Her tattoos are moving, creating new pictures across the canvas of her body. Each one is a replica of the running girl from the film—the same girl who is now on fire in the corner, blazing away silently. Like an old-fashioned flicker frame, the thin black figures run on the spot, never really going anywhere, just stuck to the woman's flesh.

The girl is now nothing but a blackened husk, a charcoal shell. The intensity of the blaze has painted the outline of her form on the white wall behind her; a cinder image, a memory that will never be erased.

You turn away and approach the door. Behind you, the woman is laughing again; she begins to speak in tongues, calling you names in a variety of languages you cannot understand.

You open the door.

Outside the room is a blasted landscape. Blackened ruins, a long dirt road, a wavering thread of fire along the horizon. You spin around and the door, along with the room beyond it, has vanished. All you can see for miles is more of the same empty, smoking landscape. In the distance, a vehicle approaches you at speed. As it gets closer, you see that it is an army jeep, but you don't recognise the decals and markings on the bodywork.

The man in the passenger seat of the jeep is holding a gun, aiming it in your direction. At this distance he might miss, but if they come any closer he'll hit you for certain.

These are trained soldiers, possibly even paid mercenaries belonging to no official army. They were taught to kill. No longer individuals, they are now part of a larger project: war as installation art; indiscriminate killing as a means of making an artistic statement.

These are not men; they are symbols, ciphers.

Meat is murder...

War is hell...

Born to kill...

Once the jeep is close enough that you can see the men are smiling and laughing, you turn around and start to run. You try to pretend that you didn't see the severed head stuck to the front of the car, impaled on a spoke of the shattered radiator grille.

When you glance down at the ground you see that you are wearing heavy army-issue boots. Your legs are clad in baggy camouflage cargo pants, and you are wearing a green shirt and combat jacket. You do not have a weapon, but there are bullets in a pouch on your belt.

A sudden burst of flames peels first the shirt and jacket and then the skin from your back. You clench your tattered fists and pump your arms and legs, trying to outrun the war—any war, whatever damned war is raging endlessly behind you.

You feel small. Tiny. Defenceless.

Up ahead of you is a naked little girl. She is running, too, and screaming. You grab her arm as you move to overtake her, pulling her up into a tight embrace. You recognise her face as she looks into your eyes, still screaming. The last time you saw her, she was ashes. You keep on going, not letting your stride falter. You need to get away; you have to save her this time.

Her screams drown out your thoughts. All you can think of is that you have to get away and protect the girl.

But there is nowhere for you to run; there is no hiding place for either of you out here, in the war zone, chased by an enemy you do not even know.

You are gripped by a terrible feeling of *déjà vu*.

This could be Vietnam, it could be Cambodia; it might be Serbia, Afghanistan, or the West Bank. It could be anywhere.

It could be anywhere at all. Any time at all.

But it is England.

It is now.

And it is happening to you.

Just as you hear the first gunshot, you see a flash of white light from a mound of rubble at the side of the road—the sun flaring off a camera lens, winking conspiratorially as you finally enter the scene and hit your mark.

A second shot rips the air apart close to your right ear. The impact ruffles your hair, shoves you sideways. You stumble, losing your grip on the girl, and feel your heart drop all the way through your body to your knees. A cry escapes your lips as you realise that you will fail her. You have already failed her.

Then all you know is explosive pain and the sense that an audience is waiting to catch you when you fall.

It ends with a man and a girl. They are no longer able to run. No music. No closing credits. Slow fade to black.

And then it starts all over again.

HARD KNOCKS

"THIS IS WHERE HE SHOT the first one." Terry pauses as he says this, as if waiting for a reaction from me. The torchlight jitters across the floor, the walls, the ceiling, showing up the decay born of disuse and neglect: warped timbers, peeling walls, broken and boarded-up windows.

"The receptionist?" I try to modulate my voice, swallowing the apprehension. I don't want him to know that I'm afraid. But this place is creepy. There's an atmosphere that can't be put into words, a sense of loss that burrows deep into my bones.

"Yeah. He came in through the main door." The torch beam swings back towards the school's main entrance and the doors Terry managed to prise open with a crowbar. "Walked up to the desk with the rifle and shot her at point-blank range in the face."

I shiver; an involuntary reaction. It is cold in here. But that's all it is: the cold, penetrating my clothing. It has already started snowing outside, the temperature has dropped down near zero, and this building is old and empty.

"Come on. Along here."

Our booted feet crunch on the rubble and broken glass scattered across the wooden floor, announcing our presence to whatever spirits might be listening. I try not to visualise patterns in the ruin, but my mind refuses to take the hint. I stay close to Terry, almost touching him, not wanting to be out of range of the arc of light cast by the torch he's carrying. "It's too quiet in here," I whisper. "Far too quiet..."

"That's because the nearest main road is a mile away. There aren't any houses close by. It's actually quite an isolated spot for a school. They say that's how he managed to get in so easily—nobody saw him until it was too late. This place is so far out of the way, nobody expected anything like that to happen, and he wasn't even questioned as he walked across the school grounds."

I remain silent, watching the darkness twitching at the edges of the torchlight, shifting and squirming as if it is composed of several living things. I have no idea what might be hiding in that darkness, and I have even less desire to find out. I only came here because he dared me to, and I like him enough to try and impress him. At least I thought I liked him. Right now, even that is unclear. I've only known him a few weeks. He could be anybody...anybody at all.

He could be crazy, for all I know.

"Shush." He stops walking, causing me to collide gently with his back.

"What is it?"

"I'm not sure... Didn't you hear that?"

I shake my head, then realise that he can't see me because I'm standing behind him. "No. What did you hear?"

He waits a couple of seconds before replying. "A sound. Like someone knocking on a door or a wall. Like a rapping sound."

"I don't like this, Terry. Can we go now?"

"Don't be fucking stupid. It's just starting to get interesting." He laughs, mocking me. "Don't tell me you never once thought about killing someone when you were at school. A bully or a teacher. Or maybe just someone who pissed you off enough to hate them." He turns to face me, shining the torch beam upwards, into his face. He doesn't look like himself. His eyes are hideously wide, his mouth is twisted into an obscene grin, and his skin looks too pale. For a second, I think about what it would be like to kill *him*. Then the thought fades, returning to wherever it came from.

"Come on. Let's go." He turns and grabs my hand, pulling me along. "It came from down here."

Reluctantly, I follow him as he leads me along a narrow corridor, closed doors on either side. "These are classrooms?" My breath mists in the air, blending with the meagre light from Terry's torch.

"That's right. He went inside, one by one, and just started shooting. As he worked his way further along the building, he started to tell whoever he found inside each room to stand facing the wall— like a punishment. He told them if they stayed where they were, and didn't try to run, they wouldn't be harmed. He said he'd stop killing."

It's still cold. Colder than before. "Jesus...and they did that? They stayed where they were, facing the wall?"

"Some of them tried to run, but he shot them in the back. The others were too scared to move. So they stood there with their eyes shut, listening to the gunshots and the screams. They were too terrified to do anything else."

I do my best to imagine them, so many kids standing in these classrooms, turned to face the wall, trying not to cry, trying not to scream; trying not to bring Edward Threshton's attention upon them so that they might live. They must have thought they had a chance. Perhaps they convinced themselves that he was telling the truth, and he'd let them go. That he wasn't just toying with them, or saving bullets.

Despite my best efforts, I cannot even begin to imagine how it might have felt to go through such a harrowing experience.

Terry slows his pace. "Here's the gym. It was pretty bad in here, according to the books and the newspaper reports." He stops outside the gym doors, staring at the dirty glass panels. "The basketball team was inside, training. He walked in, shut the door behind him, and started shooting them in the legs. A few of them died instantly because his aim was off—he got them in the head or the chest—but enough were crippled so that he could calmly tie them up and leave them there while he dealt with the others, the ones still waiting in the classrooms."

I shut my eyes. I know from my own reading that Edward went back to the classrooms and methodically shot each of the waiting students in the back, or the back of the head. Even then, too scared or still convinced that if they didn't move they might be safe, none of them had even tried to escape.

Nobody knows why he did it this way. They suspect he was simply playing games.

"Like shooting fish in a barrel," says Terry. I don't like the tone of his voice. He seems amused, as if this is all just one big joke, something that happened simply to entertain him.

"It's horrible," I say, drawing my hand away from his, making tight little fists in the dark.

"Yes...yes, it is. But it's also *fascinating*."

My patience is growing thin, lending me courage that I don't really feel. A delayed sense of outrage fills me, and then overflows. "It isn't a movie. This stuff happened. It actually happened. How can you be so fucking cold?"

This time I hear the sound immediately: a rapid knocking, three times, followed by silence.

Terry grins. "What the fuck?"

"Terry...I'm scared. I want to go."

"Then go back. Leave me here."

Turning, I face the blackness of the corridor we came along.

Again, I see vague movement, a gentle surging of darkness, like the churning of some great black sea. It's just my eyesight, I know this; the sight of all that darkness is forcing me to create images where there are none. But still, I'm unable to turn back on my own. I'm too afraid to leave.

"Don't be such a pussy." Terry reaches out and pushes open the gym doors.

The torch beam plays over the sprung wooden floor. It is flaking away in places, and there are areas where the boards have been torn up and removed to reveal the bones of bare joists beneath.

"Careful," says Terry, as he steps inside. "It might not be safe." I think he's smiling, but I can't be sure. I'm glad I can't see his face.

I follow him. What else can I do? I don't want to stand outside the gym by myself, waiting in the dark, and he is carrying the only torch. He made sure of that, damn him.

"We shouldn't have come here," I say, softly, to myself.

"But we did," says Terry. "And you can't pretend it isn't exciting."

Any vague feelings of excitement I first experienced at the idea of coming here, to the old murder school, dissipated as soon as we broke in and started exploring the tatty, empty halls. All those closed doors (Why were they left that way? Couldn't some of them have been opened?), the shut-in atmosphere, the cloying, dusty air that tickles my throat...

"Look. There are still bloodstains."

My gaze follows the beam of the torch, noting the dark patches on the wooden floor. I don't want to look, but I have no choice. He is right; the marks could be dried blood. But they could also be water damage caused by a leaking ceiling.

"I bet those areas over there, where the boards have been ripped out, were taken as mementos. Other people have been here, and they've not left empty-handed. They took souvenirs. I've seen things up for sale on eBay. Someone even claims to have got hold of some bullet casings from his rifle. How cool is that?"

I don't particularly want to touch Terry, but I can't help it. Reaching out, I grab the sleeve of his jacket. "Can we go now? You've seen it—this is where you wanted to come, isn't it—the gym, the locus, where he killed the most?"

"Shut up." He walks across the gymnasium, shining the torch into all the corners. There are a couple of old vaulting horses, the outdated climbing frames bolted to the walls, thick ropes with knotted ends dangling from the ceiling joists and casting strange shadows as they move idly in an unseen draft.

"He forced the gym teacher to hang himself from one of those." Terry stands directly beneath a swaying length of rope. His face looks...avid, hungry. That's the only way I can think of to describe his expression. "He told the teacher that if he did it, some of them would be spared. So the fucking idiot took him at his word...he climbed onto a vaulting horse, tied the rope around his neck, and stepped off. Edward stood and watched him choke to death, and then he went on with the killing."

He stares up at the rope for a long time, his eyes becoming distant, unfocused. I wish that he would stop acting this way, but I'm too afraid of him now to interrupt his reverie. Before, I'd thought it was simple curiosity that had drawn him here, but now I suspect it's something more. Terry is interested in serial killers, atrocities, random killings. He collects books and documentaries on the subject of murder. At first it made him seem interesting, not like the other guys I'd met at college. But this...this is something entirely different. I realise now that he isn't here to satisfy his idle curiosity; he has come to pay homage.

He starts speaking again: "Can you imagine the mental drive it must have taken to do this? To come here, and stay calm while you made people do exactly what you wanted them to do. The sense of control he must have felt...it must've been incredible. To wield that kind of power over someone else...it's awesome."

Behind me, I hear the knocking sound again. This time it sounds twice: two sets of three knocks. "Terry..."

He glances at me, and then looks past me, over my shoulder, at the doors through which we first entered the gym.

"I think he's here."

My skin goes cold. Every inch of it: all over my body. "What do you mean?"

"Remember when the police finally arrived, and they were talking to him from outside, through a loudhailer? They asked him why he'd done it, and all he said was 'They needed schooling.' I've thought about that for a long time." His gaze flickers back towards me, settling on my face. "He was a teacher, looking for apt pupils. But he found none, so the lesson he gave fell on deaf ears at the time. It's only now, years later, that we can learn something from what he did. I've studied his lesson, I've taken on board his schooling, and I've come to the conclusion that he's come back. School is back in session."

Slowly, I start to back away. "You're fucking insane." The boards groan beneath my feet. The darkness rushes towards me with open arms. The knocking sound comes again from behind me, further along the corridor, closer to us.

"That sound...the sound you hear. As he walked along the corridor, he knocked three times on each of the classroom doors with his rifle barrel. It was just something he did, a kind of twitch he had. Part of some OCD ritual, I suppose. According to one of the books I read, he couldn't walk past a door without knocking on it three times, ever since he was a little kid."

As if on cue, the knocking starts up again: sets of three, more of them now. And they are coming closer.

"It's sad, really, that Edward's ideal pupil should only turn up to school this long after the event." He smiles, but the darkness pours into his mouth, his eyes, his ears, making his features go dark, too. He takes a step towards me, then another. Slow, deliberate steps that I know I can never outrun, however fast I might be. The knocking sound approaches from behind me at a similar pace.

"Please, Terry. You're scaring me. I want to go home."

"There's no going home now." His smile is gaping; I can't see his teeth behind his lips, only blackness. "Teacher's coming."

That is when I hear the final three knocks, the ones on the gym door, right behind me. I stop moving, stiffen, feeling as if I'm falling towards something from which I should be running, running and not stopping.

Before me, Terry goes down on his knees. He holds up his hands in an attitude of prayer, a supplicant at the altar. His face goes slack, the expression dreamy. He closes his eyes and begins to sway.

"No," I whisper, and then feel something like a hand resting lightly on my shoulder, the fingers tightening around the trapezius muscle. Something small and hard presses firmly into the base of my back—the muzzle of a rifle, perhaps—and then, before I have time to question what is happening, I'm being pushed forward, past Terry's kneeling form, and towards the wall.

Panicking, I grab the climbing frame to try and stop from being pushed right up against it, but the pressure from behind is too much to fight. A hard body presses against my spine; hot breath coats the side of my face. I try to deny that it's there, but there's a smell like old fireworks and the air around me turns cold.

"*Stay here*," says a voice; it is soft, surprisingly tender. "*Move and I'll kill you."*

Then whoever has just spoken steps silently away.

I try not to move, not to breathe.

All is quiet now. I strain to hear something in the silence.

It doesn't take long. A single gunshot rings out inside the gym, and then a body slumps slowly to the floor. I wait for something more, but it doesn't come.

Oh, God...

I force my eyes shut tighter, grasping the climbing bars so hard that my fingers hurt. Noises: footsteps across the wooden floor, the doors slamming shut.

Please, let me live...

I listen intently to the separate sets of three knocks as they move away, back along the main corridor and towards the front of the school building, as my tormentor leaves the premises.

Stay there. That's what the voice said.

But how long should I stay here? How long precisely did he mean for me to stay put?

Move and I'll kill you.

Eventually the triple knocking sounds fade, and then they stop entirely.

Unwilling to move even an inch, and entirely unable to speak, I remain trapped in the same position, with my body pressed up against the wall-mounted climbing frame.

Time loses all meaning; the world slows to a halt. I can hear my heart beating.

Thoughts of my own childhood rise to the surface and break free. The times when I was sent out of class for being disruptive; the countless lectures I received from teachers and parents; the way I could never fit in, no matter how hard I tried or how much I wished that it could be different; the fantasies I'd once entertained about making a bomb and blowing up the school...hot, sweaty dreams of death and destruction that I would never have acted upon, even when I was pushed past my breaking point.

Do those dreams (or were they wishes?) have any bearing here, on this situation? Is there a connection of some kind between me and the boy who once turned this school into a slaughterhouse? Has my very presence here summoned some dark genie from out of his bottle?

Alternatively, this could all be a bad joke, designed by Terry to scare me. Or he might be re-enacting the horror, using me to set the scene. The truth is, I can't be sure. Of anything.

I tell myself that I will stay here for as long as it takes, whatever length of time that might eventually be, just to be sure.

Because if I don't, *he* might come back for me—just like he did for those other pupils, despite his calm promises—and my schooling will continue, as if it never ended in the first place. The next time I hear those triple-taps on the doors or the walls will be the last.

There is one thing in my favour. I was always a quick study. Throughout my life, I have learned my lessons well.

And this time I'm determined to be top of the class.

NECROPOLIS BEACH

AS FAR AS I KNOW it was one of the first incursions, those initial incidents that we now realise were merely glimpses of what was soon to come. Back then, of course, we had no idea what it meant. Nobody did. This was before the mass panic, the media blackouts, the riots, and the unstoppable rising of the sea levels. Before things whose names were horror itself started to break through for real and disassemble our world, piece by screaming piece.

This was before all of that; the intimate before the epic.

We were on a working holiday, investigating some old cave and tunnel networks found on the island of Menorca. The site was already familiar to us; we'd read about it when the original set of ruins was uncovered back in the mid-nineties. But now we knew that we needed to go there, to see the place for ourselves, because this time what they'd found was older than anything else in the area.

Deep within a small cave system, scrawled on a wall revealed by an inexplicable subterranean rockslide, one of the custodians of the site had discovered some well-preserved etchings. They depicted humanoid figures coming up out of the sea. Their limbs were long and distorted; their faces were stretched; they seemed to rise from the waters like something boneless and unused to moving on dry land.

Tina and I had spent the day looking at the etchings, photographing them, documenting the images so that we could write up a report for the funding bodies. I wasn't sure about the origin of the cave markings, but the strata down there were much older than the exposed caves above. Somebody mentioned prehistoric troglodytes and laughed. I didn't even crack a smile.

We called in using Skype, reporting our findings to the office in London. Brent, our boss, didn't seem too interested. He was blasé about the work. Years ago, he'd been passionate, a real firebrand, but these days he didn't give a shit about anything but how many days were left until he could cash in his final-salary pension.

We logged off and went to the hotel bar. There were not a lot of people around. Out of season, the island dried up, curled in on itself like a sleeping serpent. The barman was bored. After he'd finished washing glasses that were already clean, he sidled up to us and made small talk. When we told him what we did, why we were here, he perked up a little and bought us drinks.

"It must be interesting," he said. "Your job. Digging through history like that." His English was immaculate. He told us that he used to live in Essex, but came home when his student loans ran out.

"I suppose it is," said Tina, the light catching the side of her face and making it glow. She always glowed to me; she was like fire, like naked flame.

"Do you know of the Necropolis Beach?"

"Which one?"

I sat there and watched Tina as she spoke, enraptured by her casual beauty. I think even then I suspected things were coming to an end.

"*Cala Morell*: Necropolis caves."

"Ah, yes. Isn't it a bit of a tourist trap?"

The barman grinned. "Not *that* one...the other one. The beach only the locals know. The old beach." His eyes sparkled. Telling a woman like Tina something she doesn't know—watching her eyes widen in interest and her lips part with excitement—makes a man feel good.

"There are things that come up out of the water. After dark. These days there are a lot of strange things...weird events that we all take for granted."

Immediately I thought of the cave etchings, the creatures depicted on the rough rock walls.

"Tell me more." Tina leaned forward, sipped her white wine.

"A long, long time ago, before people came to this island for holidays, the indigenous Catalans had secrets. Some of those secrets remained hidden. Secrets like *sin espinas*: the boneless ones. They have returned to the beach. They've come home."

Tina laughed. It was a beautiful sound. I never stopped loving the music of her laughter, the way it bent the air to meet its demands. "*Espinas*...doesn't that mean thorns? Like on a rose?"

The barman shrugged. "I'm being serious. Here..." He grabbed a napkin and began to scribble on it with a biro pen. "This is the way. You can drive only so far, and then you must walk." He handed her the hand-drawn map.

"Really?" She stared at him. From the angle where I was sitting, I was unable to see her eyes, but I knew the expression on her face well. She would be tearing him down with her gaze, casting upon him the full force of her considerable personality.

"I swear to you," said the barman, his voice low. "You'll thank me after you see this. *Sin espinas*...the ones without bones."

We didn't go to the beach that night. Instead we drank too much local Mahon gin and stared into one another's eyes. The barman soon moved away, sensing that we were sharing something that he could not fathom, no matter how hard he tried. Tina and I stumbled back to our room, where we made love by candlelight. I remember her hands on my skin, the way her eyes reflected the lambent flame; I remember it all, and I treasure the memory.

Afterwards, as we lay holding each other, Tina said "*Espinas...* You know, I'm pretty sure that's also something to do with filleting a fish. I remember the phrase, or something like it, from a Spanish cookbook."

"Does it even matter?" I stroked her arm, enjoying the softness of her skin.

She pulled away. "I don't know. It might."

When she fell asleep, I sensed a division between us, as if something had cleaved us apart. It confused me, this feeling. I had no idea what had happened to cause such a negative sensation. For months now, we had been drifting apart. It had been a gradual thing: slow, incremental movements rather than major seismic shifts.

I lay awake for a little while, and then the shadows closed in. The last thing I thought about before drifting into them was the image of a fish without bones, but with large curved thorns sticking out of its flesh.

The next day we were back on site, cataloguing and documenting, doing our jobs. We uncovered more of the drawings, this time showing the boneless figures raising their floppy arms into the air as if calling down something from above. Peeling back layers of dirt, we saw more and more of these painstakingly scored images. The pictures began to unnerve me. There was something wrong, but I couldn't quite focus in on what it was. Perhaps it had something to do with the unvoiced tension between Tina and me, or maybe it was something in the air—a sense of impending change.

We ate an early dinner in a small hillside restaurant, then drove back down to the hotel. The barman who'd given us the map wasn't there. It must have been his night off. We almost didn't bother going. I tried to convince us both that he'd been trying to impress her, flirting by relating some silly local myth as if it were the truth.

Tina wouldn't listen. She wanted to go down to the secret beach. "What's the worst that could happen? There's nothing there, so we fuck on the sand and come back here for a nightcap."

She could always convince me to join her on an adventure. I was powerless whenever she spoke to me that way.

We drove down to the coast in our little rental car, following the directions on the sketchy paper-napkin map. I almost missed the turn-off. The road was typically narrow and winding; the trees hung down onto the blacktop near the verge. At the last minute I saw a sign: *Cala Morell*. I stepped on the brake and managed to turn in. Stopped the car at an angle.

I got out and looked around, moving away from the road that led down to the little cove where the tourists went to look at the burial holes gouged into the cliff face, the ones featured in all the holiday brochures. Just as the barman had said, the alternative route was hard to find; also as he'd said, I did find it eventually. Pulling back some low-hanging branches, I caught sight of a narrow footpath that in reality could barely even be called that. It was merely a line of flattened undergrowth, a casual pathway where feet had trod in the past.

"This way," I said, turning. But she was already standing right behind me, smiling.

After a few minutes following the dark route, the trees and bushes began to thin out and we saw torchlight up ahead. Several people were making their way down the same rough path. As we neared them, we saw even more up ahead. Tina seemed disappointed, but I was glad: I didn't want us to be the only people down there if anything did come up out of the sea.

We walked hand in hand, part of the crowd: this solemn procession of strangers moving together through the darkness towards a common goal.

The barman had told us that the pathway was 2km long from the crude entrance down to the beach. It ran downhill at a steep gradient—which meant the return journey would be tiring—and now that we'd travelled a while and the undergrowth had receded, I could identify that the surface was basically a sandy dirt track set in a cutting between two high cliffs.

Nobody spoke; the silence was respectful, even reverent. It felt as if we were taking part in a holy pilgrimage of some kind.

Tina squeezed my hand, looking for reassurance. I turned my head, surprised at her newfound trepidation, and smiled. She smiled back, but coyly, as if she barely knew me. We carried on down the narrow track, bamboo trees rising up on either side of us. The people with flashlights lit the way for the rest of us. It would have been impossible to drive a vehicle of any kind along this route, even one of the mopeds the islanders favoured. The track was rutted, its surface uneven. I was worried that Tina might slip and fall because she was wearing her cheap flip-flops. I watched the bobbing heads in front of us, the spidery limbs in the futile flash of electric lights that spilled across the landscape. Somebody sneezed. A woman started to say something and then changed her mind.

"This is exciting," said Tina. "I wonder why this isn't better known—you'd think it would be mentioned in the guide books or something."

"Imagine what it would be like with a horde of tourists tramping down this crappy path. Remember what that guy said: the islanders have their secrets." I shrugged.

"I suppose so," said Tina. "It's more exciting this way, too, like we're all in on something special." When she smiled, light splashed across her face for a moment before twitching away to illuminate something else.

Before long we came to the beach. Virgin sand. A tiny natural bay. Tide-sculpted rocks and two decaying rowing boats tied to the shore with frayed ropes. There was a salty tang of rot in the air. Far up on the cliff faces to the left and right of us, I could just about make out the prehistoric burial chambers carved out of the rock: a series of shallow caves, each with a shelf inside that had been used to store a body. Dangerous-looking staircases—also carved from pure rock—snaked up and along the cliffs. I had no desire to climb them.

Wooden torches lined the small shoreline. A couple of men began to light them. I could smell the petrol; the bundled rags at the end of each wooden stake had already been doused in fuel. Flames caught; light wavered; the sea lapped gently against the rocks.

Those at the front of the group, nearest the shore, got down on their knees facing the water. The rest of us followed suit; a weird Mexican wave of kneeling people.

"It won't be long," someone whispered in heavily-accented English. "They'll know we're here. They always do."

Then, once again, silence descended.

The advance group was spotted several minutes later—a large luminous blanket floating in the shallows, heading purposefully towards the shore. I watched in a kind of numbed awe as the initial shoal came out of the sea and flopped onto the sand. They seemed to possess the rudimentary shape of humans, but they were gelatinous, squashy and boneless, like jellyfish. What had been graceful in the water was clumsy on dry land; they flapped and writhed across the sand, limbs twitching, sightless faces turned moonward. Camera flashes flared, breaths were held, eyes widened. More things emerged from the sea to join the others. Soon nine or ten of them had come ashore.

"*Sin espinas,*" someone whispered.

"They're beautiful," said Tina, and for a moment I thought she was joking. But when I looked at her, I could see her eyes reflecting the flames. She was mesmerised by these things; she couldn't look away, even if she wanted to. And clearly she didn't.

The things squirmed closer, and then they paused in their movement, raising their rubbery arms up towards the sky. Each one turned up its jellied face and looked into the star-strung blackness, opening its mouth as if to scream, or perhaps to relay a silent summons to whatever was up there, waiting to be called.

Fear gripped me, but I had no idea why.

I reached out to take Tina's limp hand, but she turned to me, smiled, and shook her head, slipping her soft, cold fingers out of my palm.

"I'm sorry. I have to go."

It was the last thing she ever said to me, so quietly that I could barely make out the words. Her voice was so inconsequential, so insufficient. It wasn't much of a note on which to end a twenty-year marriage.

"Don't go." But it was already too late; it was much too late, because she'd already left me. I'd known for months that whatever we had once shared was over. We were both simply waiting for the right moment to admit the truth. When we'd made love the night before, it had felt like goodbye. I didn't want to admit it at the time, but right then I had no choice. All truth was revealed: a light shone into my depths and I felt empty.

As Tina stood and slowly made her way through the kneeling onlookers towards the night surf, a respectful round of applause started up. There were no words, just this soft clapping—a polite appreciation of what she was doing. I joined in, unable to do anything else. I still don't know why I didn't go after her, drag her back up that steep pathway to the car, and drive us both away. It crossed my mind—of course it did—but for some reason the actions seemed inappropriate, as if I might offend something bigger and much more important than my own earthly needs and desires.

It was at that point I noticed the barman among the onlookers. He smiled sadly. I held his gaze for a moment and then looked away, back towards my wife.

Tina had shed her clothes as she approached the water. Her skin shone in the darkness, supplying its own luminescence. The unsteady things on the shore managed to turn themselves around and follow her back into the sea, as if she had always been the one to lead them.

Twisting at the waist, she looked back at me one final time and smiled. But I couldn't read the smile at all; it was one I'd never seen before, weak and tragic and entirely inscrutable.

I tried to call out to her, but whatever had a hold on me wouldn't let me speak. I continued slow-clapping, hating myself for allowing my actions to be dictated by another, unseen, consciousness.

The last I saw of Tina was her long, pale back arching in the moonlight as she dove beneath the grey waves, and then she was gone. Even the ripples vanished quickly. I tried to remember her face but all I could picture was the way she parted her hair, the smudged shadows under her eyes, the way she turned away from me, shaking her head, whenever I said something stupid.

I was the last one to leave the beach that night.

People patted me on the shoulder, ruffled my hair, or simply paused for a moment to look down at me before they left. One or two of them even took my photograph.

When finally I was alone, I stood up and walked down to the shoreline and stood on the rocks looking outward. The sea was dark and quiet. The caves above and around me held more than the weighted darkness of ancient pre-history. The last vestige of some older force was stirring, possibly even waking.

After what seemed like aeons, I turned around and walked away from the shore, knowing that I would never come back here, to this hidden beach, or even to this beautiful island, where once I'd been close to happiness with the woman I loved.

Come morning, when Tina's rubbery bones washed up on the shore or were deposited like lifeless anemone in a series of shallow rock pools by the retreating tide, I would be long gone. Let them be gathered up by strangers and taken to whatever museum was used to house such artefacts. I needed no memento or keepsake of this ridiculous nighttime ritual. I knew even then it was simply the beginning of something greater; the first throes of a cosmic convulsion that would tear the world apart. But the truth was that Tina had already abandoned me a long time ago. Everything else was just the aftermath.

By the time I reached the car, whatever strange hold the beach seemed to have on me had dissipated. I climbed inside the vehicle, lowered my forehead to the steering wheel, and wept.

This memory would be all I had left to comfort me during the many bad times ahead: the soft touch of an already jelly-like hand, a weak smile in the darkness, white skin sinking beneath dark waters, the sound of the sea gently lapping at the time-smoothed rocks...

Wherever she is now, and whatever she has become, I pray that Tina knows I still love her. I always will.

TETHERED DOGS

HE LOOKED AT HIS EMPTY glass, a confused expression on his face. "I can't even remember drinking that."

I turned to Ledley, motioned for him to pour Joel another pint, and then took a mouthful of wonderfully hot, bitter coffee. Waited for him to tell me what was on his mind.

"We've known each other in passing for a few years, right?"

"Yeah. That's right."

"I don't think we've ever had a conversation that lasted longer than a quick hello before now, have we?"

I shook my head. "Not that I recall, no. I suppose that would make us what they call 'nodding acquaintances.'"

He smiled again. I wished he'd stop doing that. It was making me feel nauseous.

"I don't have a lot of close friends. Not real ones. You know something of what I do for a living, yeah?"

"It's none of my business what you do."

"But you do know...you know I'm a bad man."

"We're all bad men in some way. I don't believe in white hats and good guys. That shit's for kids."

I think he'd already decided he was going to tell me his story. Nothing I said could have altered that.

He clenched his fists on the table and then eased off the pressure, slowly opening his hands. "Something weird happened tonight. I'm going to tell you about it so I don't have to keep it inside my head. This is something I need to share, if only for my own sanity."

"Give me a second." I got up and collected his drink from the bar. Ledley didn't say anything, just stared at me as he pretended to clean glasses. When I returned to the booth it looked like Joel had been trying not to cry. His eyes were red but there were no tears.

"Here." I pushed the pint of ale towards him.

"Thanks, man." Joel drank half the contents in one swallow and then put down the glass.

"You know me, Joel. I'm not going to judge you. I've done a lot of bad things myself, so I can claim no moral high ground. We're just two blokes sitting in a pub and having a chat."

He blinked once, slowly, as if he was trying to clear his vision, and then continued. "One of my girls tried to kill herself tonight. She climbed onto the roof behind my place and jumped. I saw her do it. Her neck snapped when she hit the ground. Sounded like a gunshot."

"Who was it?"

"Jenny Dope."

"The little junkie girl from Marsh Street? I know her. She's the one whose kid died in that road accident, isn't she?"

"Yeah. Six months ago, now. But it was no accident. A hit and run. Nobody ever found the guy who did it." He stared at me and I knew that, contrary to popular belief, someone *had* found him, but nobody else would ever know where the body was buried.

"Okay. Say no more."

"Jenny couldn't deal with the loss. She'd gone rapidly downhill, taking more drugs, stronger ones, and treating herself badly."

"Yeah, I heard a bit about that. Someone told me recently that she was selling herself for a hit from a dirty needle in some squat in East

Leeds."

"I was trying to wean her off that shit. I took her out of that hovel and gave her a room. Thought I was actually getting somewhere. Until tonight."

"So, she's dead?"

"Kind of."

His answer hit me right under the ribs, almost winding me. I didn't know how to respond, so I said nothing. I wished that I hadn't sat down with him in the first place but by then it was too late to get up and go.

"Her neck snapped. Head was twisted all the way around—literally all the way—so that she was staring backwards. She wasn't breathing. I checked. Her heart wasn't beating. I checked that too. She should've been a goner. Should've, but wasn't. Not quite."

In the depths of the brief silence that followed, when he stopped speaking and simply stared at me, I sensed so many things that should remain unknown. I smelled the hint of decay, heard a silent scream on the wind, felt the presence of someone or some*thing* I knew I'd meet again, face to face, on my death bed.

"She was dead, but she was still speaking. I don't know how, or why. With her head turned back-to-front, she was gabbling, talking a lot of shit. Me and one of the boys carried her back inside and put her on a bed in one of the back rooms, the ones we don't let the customers use. The rooms where the girls can go for a rest and grab a bit of privacy. Clean sheets, new carpets, painted nice and bright. We had to lay her down on her front so that she was face-up. Her eyes were open, but you could tell she couldn't see us. I have no idea what she was looking at..."

The jukebox in the corner started playing an old song, but I couldn't focus clearly enough to make out the words. All I could think of was this young girl with her head facing the wrong way, dead but still managing to speak.

"The thing is, she kept on talking. Couldn't stop. She kept up this strange monologue, reciting names and dates and causes of death. It took us a little while to realise that she was giving us the death dates of everyone she knew. Then she moved on to other things—predictions. She told us that ten years from now there'll be a terrorist attack on the Houses of Parliament. Next week a family of six will be killed in a house fire in Sheffield. Stuff like that...and some things I can't even bring myself to repeat."

"Then what happened?"

"I had to get the hell out of there, so I came here. I needed a drink, and to be in the company of real people. We didn't call the police or the ambulance service—I mean, what the fuck was I meant to tell them? How do you explain a dead woman with her head twisted a hundred and eighty degrees on her neck predicting death and destruction? It's crazy. They'd think I was insane."

"So she's still there?"

He nodded. "We locked her in the room. You can still hear her droning on behind the door in that flat, lifeless voice. I don't know what to do."

Neither did I. None of us ever knows what to do in times of great duress, but something always comes up. And round here I'm usually the one who comes up with it.

"Show me," I said, and I have no idea why. It was none of my business. I didn't want to get involved. Yet I stood and followed him out of the Gut Punch, walked half a mile to his place on a quiet street that backs onto fields grown wild with neglect. The night was warm, the air was clear. I could see every star in the firmament; if I'd wanted to, I could have counted each one of them and given them names.

"Come on. This way." He opened the door and we walked along a short corridor, bedrooms branching off it, doors shut tight in their frames. I don't think there were customers behind any of those doors. Joel must have shut up shop after the last one left, his balls and wallet emptied.

We went into the kitchen of the converted house. A middle-aged woman sat in her underwear at the dining table, drinking tea. She didn't look up at us as we passed through; her mind was on other matters. A thin young man with a bad complexion stood at her side, staring at the top of her head as if he could find the secret of existence within her greasy blonde curls.

I don't think either of them was even aware of us being there.

We left them behind. For a moment it felt like I was leaving everything behind. Those people, this house, my life...all of it.

Joel stopped outside a door at the end of a second narrow corridor. He stood and stared at the door, as if he were trying to wish it away or convince himself that it wasn't really there, that a solid wall had appeared in its place. "She's in here," he said, reaching out a hand and placing his palm against the painted timber. "We didn't know what else to do."

As I watched, he took a set of keys from his jacket pocket. Examining them, he selected one and used it to unlock the door. I could hear mumbling from inside the room. When he opened the door, the voice became clearer. It sounded like chanting, or a repeated prayer.

Joel stepped through the door and then to one side, giving me a view of the room. The walls were painted bright yellow; the carpet was clean and white. Pretty curtains hung at the small window. Flowers in a vase on the windowsill. I could smell lavender air-freshener. There was a wardrobe, a small chest of drawers, a neat double bed.

On the bed was a woman. She was small and thin and wearing a pair of tight black jeans and a faded Motörhead tour t-shirt. No shoes or socks. She had tiny feet, small nubs of toes. Her arms were bruised. Her neck was twisted in a kind of fleshy spiral and she lay on her belly, but face-up, talking non-stop. Her voice was quiet, but she wasn't quite whispering. It sounded like an old recording: flat, distant, lacking tone and timbre.

I didn't want to hear what she was saying. Names, dates, numbers, causes of death. It sounded like she was reading from a list.

"She hasn't stopped. She won't. She just keeps on talking and telling us these things...and we don't know what to do."

I remembered this girl from before, when she used to push a pram through the park and pick wildflowers to put in her baby's hair. She'd been as happy as anyone I'd ever seen, but even then, she'd been using and working occasionally in Joel's grotty little suburban whorehouse. The shadows were already gathering; darkness had never been far from her side.

I'd walked into a trap. Joel was relinquishing all responsibility for this girl by bringing me here. He knew enough about me to be certain I'd do the right thing, the thing that he couldn't bring himself to do.

It was always the same. People dragged me into their business and expected me to sort it out. I've spent my life cleaning up other people's messes, and don't expect things to change any time soon. They seek me out. It's like a mark upon my skin, a stain on my flesh. They can see it when they look at me—they know I can never turn them down when they come to me for help.

We all have our roles to play, and this, it appears, is mine.

I felt like punching Joel in the face, but I knew that if I got started on that I might not stop until I'd killed him. He looked pathetic, standing in the corner with his eyes shining and his shoulders stooped. He was already a beaten man; anything that I could have done would have added little to his current sense of defeat.

It was then that I realised what he must have been told by the girl on the bed: the date of his own death, and how it would come about. I wondered if she'd told him he would be murdered, or if he would go quietly in his sleep. Would he die young or old? If he was to be murdered, had she named his killer?

These are the things that we can never know, for it will break our minds; the secret knowledge we must not be told. We dance through life unaware of the date of our own extinction. It's the only thing that stops us from losing our sanity. To know that—to be informed of it with such unwavering certainty—is surely the definition of hell on earth.

I turned my attention back to the girl on the bed. Did she know that I was here? I didn't want her to tell me anything about myself. A bell, once struck, can't be unrung. A scream cannot be unheard.

Quickly, quietly, I stepped forward and stood by the bed, staring down at Jenny Dope. Her eyes were wide open, but she couldn't see a thing. She wouldn't even know it was happening. Her shoulder blades were sharp beneath the thin material of her t-shirt; her spine was prominent. She looked used up, wasted.

I reached down and clasped her head, a hand on each side of her small, sweaty skull, and twisted hard, turning her head back the right way. The bones grated; blood spurted from her mouth as she coughed involuntarily, staining the pillow red. She stopped speaking mid-sentence. I was glad she hadn't yet said my name.

I left her lying face-down on the bed, silent at last.

Joel tried to follow me out of the room as I left, but I turned and pushed him away. He was smart enough to stay where he was. The couple in the kitchen were standing, locked in a loose embrace, as I walked through the room and towards the front door. It looked like they were slow-dancing to a tune only they could hear.

Outside, everything was the same as it always had been. Nothing had changed. The sky was still above me, the earth remained solid beneath my feet. My life was a mess, my job was pointless, and my children were still on the other side of the world, growing up without me in their lives.

I heard a song comprising of distant sirens and the barking of tethered dogs as I headed back to the Gut Punch, not knowing where else to go. It was the best home I had, the only one I knew. When I got there, I stood outside the building and stared up at the roof, wondering how long it would take me to climb up to its highest level, and how far I might see when I got there.

The journey would be much quicker on the way back down.

Jenny Dope had known that better than anyone, even at the end.

I stayed there for a long time until finally, feeling tired and useless and sick of myself, I stalked away into the muggy northern night, looking for something I would never find. Searching for something—anything—that I could pretend was better than this.

THE HANGING BOY

PAUL WALKED SLOWLY TO THE edge of the embankment
and looked down at the abandoned railway line. Most of the old timber
sleepers had rotted away long ago; long grass had grown up in the gaps
between the brittle remains, as stiff and dry as dead men's hair.
Random pieces of the metal track had survived, but they were old and
rusted.

He stood for a while, enjoying what passed for silence out here at
the outskirts of town, the edge of nothing. The main road was too far
away to be heard; the town centre was even more distant. All he could
hear was birdsong and the low rustling of small animals making their
way through the undergrowth.

There followed a moment of peace in which he reflected, in an
unfocused adolescent way, upon his life: the arguments his parents had
when they'd been drinking, the beatings dished out to him when he
didn't do as he was told, and the long hours spent on his own because
none of the other neighbourhood kids seemed to like him.

But here, in this quiet place, it was different. Out here he could
imagine something better.

He could pretend that he was the last person on earth: a young
boy left behind when everyone else died of some disease or boarded a
spaceship bound for another planet, colonists on a journey into the
darkness.

But the fantasy never lasted. The rest of the world was always there, at his back. No matter how hard he tried to ignore it. Reality always crept back in, despite his best attempts to keep it at bay.

Carefully, he made his way down the embankment and stepped softly onto the line. He paused for a moment, looking back along the decrepit railway line and into the distant past. Trains had stopped running here a long time before he was born. The factories that required the railway for haulage were all shut down, the workers dismissed. He could not detect even an echo of what was here before.

He shrugged and carried on, crossing the line, and as he did so something around him seemed to shift, as if he was passing from one atmosphere into another. The experience was difficult to define, so he didn't bother; he simply dismissed the sensation and continued walking towards the trees on the other side of the railway cutting.

It was dim between the tree trunks. They stood close and tall, unchecked by human hands and left to grow wild. Shadows pooled at the bases of the tree trunks, where the roots resembled rough brown serpents. Leftover rainwater was cupped in the leaves of the plants growing near the ground. He could smell decay, the slow rotting of everything around him.

The sounds of animals moving around in the undergrowth were louder here, and more numerous. Paul had no idea how many different kinds of species he shared this place with, but he didn't feel at all threatened by any of them. Nature did not hate him. Only people seemed to do that.

Continuing deeper into the trees, rising up the opposite embankment and heading towards a spot he knew from other visits, he allowed himself to relax and enjoy the sense of freedom. No parents arguing, no baby sister demanding attention, no evenings spent hiding away in his room so he could be left alone to read or draw or simply think about what might lie ahead of him in the hazy future.

He liked to come here, to this isolated railway cutting, because everyone else tended to ignore it. The place was too far away for the other kids to bother with, and he'd never seen any evidence of the local junkies or drunks or vagrants. It was just him and the hills and the woods; nothing more and nothing less.

He cleared the top of the rise and headed east. After a short while he came to a natural clearing. At the centre of the clearing there stood a big old oak tree. He knew this tree well, had sat beneath it reading comics, napping, or daydreaming about the pretty girls at school who barely even noticed his existence.

Paul looked up into the branches and caught sight of something hanging there.

It took a little while to process what he saw, but eventually his brain digested the information and identified the sight: the scratched soles of brown leather shoes and a glimpse of thick woollen socks beneath the ends of dirty trouser legs with rolled-up cuffs.

Small feet. A pair of skinny legs. A body, dangling. A boy.

There was a boy hanging from the branches of the tree.

Paul backed up a little so he could gain a better vantage point, his feet whispering softly in the grass, the hems of his trousers getting damp. The boy had a rope noose tied around his neck; he was suspended from a sturdy branch by the ragged noose.

Paul started to turn away, horrified, or pretending to be horrified. The difference between the two states was so tiny that it failed to matter. None of his emotions made sense. He had no idea how he was supposed to react to something like this.

"Don't go."

He looked up again at the hanging boy.

"Please. Stay for a little while."

Paul took a shuffling few steps forward, towards the tree. The boy. "Hello?"

"Hi." The boy raised a small white hand—his right hand—and waggled his fingers in a little waving gesture. His legs swayed gently; an eerie mid-air dance.

"This is impossible," said Paul.

"It can't be. If it's happening, it can't be impossible, can it?"

Paul didn't know what to do or say, so he stood and watched, waiting for a prompt.

The boy spoke again, proving that he wasn't a figment of Paul's imagination: "I'm lonely. It would be nice to have some company for a little while." He swung his legs; his feet described small circles in the air above Paul's head. His smile was pleasant.

"What are you doing up there?"

"Nothing much. Just hanging around."

They both laughed. Paul couldn't help it. The joke was funny. It broke the ice; the tension between them was thinning, evaporating. This wasn't so bad. It was becoming more real by the second. Maybe Paul had finally found a friend.

"Seriously...what are you doing?"

"I don't know. Not really. I just dangle up here, waiting."

"Waiting for what?"

"I don't know." The boy shook his head. "I honestly don't know. I'm just waiting."

Paul scratched his cheek: not because it was itchy, but as a gesture to steady his nerves. It was something to do with his hands. "How long have you been there?"

"For as long as I can remember. When I came up here, the trains were still running. The factories belched smoke into the sky. The cars were old and the houses were new. Everything was different."

"That's a long time, I think." Paul had no idea how long exactly, but he knew it must be more than a few years; decades, perhaps. "How do you keep track of time?"

"I just do." The boy flexed his hands, as if they were stiff and he was trying to get the circulation going. "That's never been a problem. I take note of the seasons." His voice was soft, with no discernible accent, as if the rough edges had been shaved off with a decent education.

"Don't you ever get bored?"

"Oh no...never. There's so much to see from up here. It's the best view in the world. The best view *of* the world. I can see it all. The changes. The advances people make. The way everything moves forward all the time, without ever pausing to catch a breath. It's fascinating. It really is."

Paul sat down on the ground and crossed his legs, right over left. He placed one hand on each knee, palms down, the fingers splayed. "Don't you get scared at night? In the dark, I mean. When it's dark."

The boy laughed; the sound was so light that it seemed to float away into the air above him. "I never get scared of anything. Being up here, it gives you a better view of things, the way they are. Now I know there's nothing to be scared of. Nothing down there can hurt me up here."

Paul stared up at the boy, not saying anything for a while. He watched as the boy cleared his throat and spat down onto the ground, and as he spun around on his noose, in slow semi-circles, first one way and then the other.

"What's your name?"

The boy tilted his head, thinking, before he answered. "I...I don't know. I think I've forgotten. I must have had a name once, I'm sure. I mean, everybody does, don't they?"

Paul nodded, and then changed the subject, not wanting to upset the boy. "Is it really good up there?"

"Yes," said the boy. "It is. It's really, really good."

"Don't you ever want to come down?"

The boy paused again, considering Paul's question, as if he had not even considered it as an option until now. "I can't say I've ever had the urge. I might have thought about it ages ago, when I was first here, but not in a long time. I like it up here. But, now that you mention it... Yes, it would be nice to stretch my legs, I suppose. It would be good to walk around for a bit, feel the ground beneath my feet for a change."

Directly above them, a thick band of clouds drifted past. The sky was grey with the threat of more rain.

"Are you hungry? I can bring you some food."

The boy shook his head. "Oh, I'm never hungry. The birds bring me things. They perch on my shoulders and feed me, putting seeds and flowers and berries on my tongue. It's like a Disney cartoon." He laughed again, and his laughter was wonderful—light and melodious and filled with an emotion Paul could not name because he didn't think he'd ever experienced it before.

"I think I'd like to climb up that tree."

The boy stopped laughing, looking down at Paul. "Is that so?"

"Yes. I think I would. Just for a little while. I'd like to get away from stuff, to hide up there in the branches where nobody can get to me. I bet that would be nice. I bet it's great."

The boy said nothing; he dangled there, so unobtrusive that he seemed like a ghost.

Is that what he was—a phantom? Paul thought it would make sense, but he wasn't afraid. There was no danger here, not from the boy.

"We could swap, if you want. I'd love to see what you see from way up there, and you could have some exercise. Go for a little jog or something."

"Oh," said the boy. "I don't know about that. *They* might not like it if I left my spot."

"Who might not like it?" Paul glanced around the clearing, wondering if someone was watching them, suddenly aware of how exposed and vulnerable he was down on the ground while the boy was safe way up there in the branches.

"I dunno. They. Whoever it was put me up here, I suppose. There must have been someone, at some point. I don't think I climbed up here by myself. At least I don't remember doing that..."

"Do you know who it was?" Paul was suddenly aware of the shadows hovering close to the ground, the hugeness of the sky, the isolation of this particular location, and the distance between him and his home. The home he didn't really want to go back to—and this was the first time he had truly confronted such a terrible thought, but it didn't disturb him. Who would even notice if he failed to return home? His uncaring mother? His violent father? The sister who was barely even old enough to have a proper identity?

"No. Like I said, I can't remember much from before. All I remember is being here, up in this tree. It feels like I didn't really have a life before that. Like I didn't start living until I was here."

Paul stood and rose onto his tiptoes. "Doesn't it hurt? The noose? Does it hurt your neck? It looks painful..."

The boy lifted one hand and touched the noose, gently, almost lovingly. "No. Not at all. I can barely even feel it. My voice sounds okay, doesn't it? Not gravelly or anything?"

Paul nodded. "Yes," he said. "It sounds fine."

"Then I guess it isn't causing me any damage." He smiled down on Paul's head. His teeth were white, almost dazzling against the dark canopy of leaves and branches.

Paul bounced on his toes. "Come on. Let's swap. Just for a bit; half an hour. It'll be fun."

The boy shrugged, or tried to, with his neck stuck in that noose. "You'd have to climb up here first and let me down."

Paul looked around him again, checking that they were still alone. All he saw were the trees, the grass, the rocks and the flowers. "That's fine. I can climb that tree easy. Just you wait and see."

He walked briskly to the thick base of the trunk, selected some firm handholds, and began to climb. As expected, it was easy for someone as lithe as him; there were many places to put his hands and feet, and the rough trunk was solid so it supported his weight. He barely registered the time it took to climb, he seemed to do it so quickly. Before long, he was up in the branches, level with the boy— within touching distance.

"Hi," said the boy.

"Hello," said Paul, examining the boy's face. Up close, it looked different. There were deep lines on his pallid forehead, wrinkles at the corners of his eyes and mouth, and his brown hair was dusty. His lips were dry, the skin peeling. There were gaps where teeth should be, despite the fact that they had looked so clean and white from the ground. His eyes were cloudy, as if the lenses needed wiping.

A thought crossed his mind: *Everything looks different up here...*

"Are you sure about this?" The boy's lips trembled.

"Yes," said Paul, not even knowing if the statement were true. "Yes, I'm certain." But he wasn't, not of anything. His life was nothing but uncertainty.

The boy reached out for him, the branches creaking with the motion. The birds stopped singing. The boy was grabbing, struggling, kicking his legs and twisting his hips so that he could take hold of

Paul's arms and wrap his legs around Paul's waist—

— and then, in a moment that seemed to exist somewhere outside of the rest of time, Paul was the one hanging in the branches, the rope noose wound tightly around his neck, like a scarf.

He had no idea how they had changed places. It seemed to happen when he wasn't looking.

Paul grabbed at the noose, grasping the big knot, trying to push his shaking fingers between the rough length of rope and his smooth, soft neck, but there was no gap between hemp and flesh.

Slowly, he stopped panicking, bringing himself back under control, and gazed out across the treetops. He could see the embankment he'd come down, the wide fields beyond, the narrow streets beyond those, and even further in the distance he could make out the roads that led into town.

It didn't hurt. The boy was right about that.

But the insight from earlier had been misleading: none of this was any different. It was the same as before. The sky was still grey, the roofs of the houses were still damp from yesterday's rain, the light still reflected dully from the glass in so many closed doors and windows.

Everything was the same.

Nothing had changed.

Paul looked at his feet.

He thought he might like to get down now and trade places again. Go back home to his drunken parents, his mother's moods, his father's fists, his needy baby sister; back to the life that had always felt so small and empty, yet now felt like it might be something worth clinging to after all.

He looked down again, along his short body, between his swinging legs, and to the hard ground, where only moments earlier he'd sat and talked with someone whose existence had not at first seemed possible.

The ground that now looked so far away, like another world.

He scanned the surrounding area, hoping to see a familiar smiling figure.

But the hanging boy was no longer there.

He was up here.

He always had been.

LITTLE BOXES

JACK DIDN'T WANT TO GO to school that morning. He didn't want to go to school *any* morning. But Jack was a good boy, so when his alarm went off he slid out of bed and padded out of the room, along the hall, to the bathroom. He brushed his teeth, showered, used the toilet, and then went back to his room to get dressed.

He put on his school uniform and looked at himself in the mirror. There was nothing remarkable about him; he was a normal eleven-year-old schoolboy with messy hair and pale skin and a family that hated him.

When he went back out into the hall, he glanced at his mum's room. Her door was slightly open. He could see the edge of the bed, and Uncle Pete's feet sticking out of the covers. Jack sighed and went downstairs.

In the kitchen, he made himself two slices of toast, slathered them with strawberry jam, and poured a glass of milk. He watched *Adventure Time* while he ate. He liked that show; it was his favourite. It made him smile. Not many things did that, so this was to be treasured.

When he'd finished his breakfast, he took the dirty dishes through into the kitchen, loaded them into the dishwasher along with last night's dishes, and then set the machine running. He stared at the dishwasher door, wishing that it was this easy to clean away the dirt from a life. After a few minutes, he turned away, grabbed his jacket off the back of a kitchen chair, and headed for the back door.

He opened the door with his key and stepped outside. On the small concrete patio, positioned below the doorstep, was a small cardboard box. Jack glanced up and then down the narrow private lane. The allotments were at the top; the main road, with the park opposite, was at the bottom. A bus trawled past the mouth of the lane. A woman pushing a pram walked by without looking in his direction.

Jack bent over and picked up the box. It was very light, much lighter than he expected; as light as a feather. He carried it back inside and set it down on the kitchen table. There was an address label stuck to the side:

Jack Finch

6 Parkview Lane

Shedley

West Yorkshire

That was all. No return address. No other identifying mark. Jack wasn't expecting a package. He hadn't ordered anything from Amazon, and it wasn't his birthday for another two months. Who would send him something? He wracked his brain, trying to identify a possible source, but nothing came.

He ran a hand over the cardboard. It felt smooth, and he detected a slight chill. He checked his watch and saw that if he didn't leave soon he was going to be late for school. Idly, he picked at the lid of the box with his fingers, but the flaps didn't budge. They must be glued down.

Shrugging, Jack left the house and started on his twenty-minute walk to school. He would take a look at the box later, when he had more time. The way things were lately, it wouldn't be anything. Or perhaps it was a box full of dog shit sent to him by Terry Nicks, the boy who'd been bullying him for over a year. He wouldn't put it past the prick. It was exactly the type of thing he'd find funny.

As he walked to school, Jack's mind drifted back to the box. He wished he'd stayed behind to open it, but if his mum or Uncle Pete had found him hanging back from school, he might have received another slap. It was happening a lot lately, since Uncle Pete had moved in with them. The man was always busy with his hands—running them all over Mum, sticking them in Jack's spare-change jar, or slapping them both around. Mum didn't seem to mind too much; she said it was better than being alone. Things had been different before Jack's dad had been killed in Afghanistan. They'd been happy, just the three of them; a happy little family, with no slapping, no money-stealing, and no nameless fears stalking them around the house like ghosts.

Jack wished that he could turn back time to put things right. He wished that his dad would appear at the door one day, still alive, and it had all been a terrible mistake. He wished that he could change things.

He walked through the school gate, instinctively looking out for Terry Nicks and his gang of hangers-on. When he walked across the playground, nodding at friendly faces and not making direct eye contact with neutral or unfriendly ones, he finally saw his own little group huddled by the gym wall.

"Jack!" Lisa waved as he approached, her small, freckled face breaking out into a grin, and then changing back to a frown.

"Hi, guys." Jack shucked off his rucksack and set it down on the ground against the wall.

"Did you get one?" asked Bill, without preamble, his pudgy face displaying a frightened expression.

"What are you on about?"

"In the post," said Scott, his skinny, nervy frame never still for a moment. "This morning. Did you get a box?"

Jack stared at his three friends. "How did you know I got something in the post?"

"An educated guess," said Lisa, moving towards him, her shoulder brushing his.

"We all got one," said Bill. "So we thought you probably did, too."

"Okay..." Jack sat down on the ground, leaning his back against the wall. "What is all this? Is it a joke?"

"We don't know," said Scott, dropping down into a squat beside him. "Did you try to open your box?"

Jack shook his head. "Didn't have time. I was running late."

"They won't open." Bill kicked the wall with the toe of his shoe. "They're stuck."

Jack smiled, but he felt uncomfortable. "What do you mean, they won't open?" He remembered how the cardboard flaps hadn't budged.

"I dunno..." Bill blew air though his mouth, causing his chubby cheeks to inflate like twin balloons. "We all tried, but we couldn't get the cardboard to tear, or even pierce it with a knife."

"I tried that," said Scott. "It was like trying to stab a sheet of metal."

Jack stood up and took a step away from the wall. "This is stupid. I'm not getting this, not any of it."

His three friends said nothing. They just stared at him, as if they expected him to solve the mystery.

At break time they were due to meet again, in their usual place against the gym wall, but Jack was sidetracked by Terry Nicks chasing him through the corridors towards the main hall. Jack hid in a storage cupboard and wondered what was going on. His friends weren't the type to make practical jokes, and they would never lie to him. They were his best mates; the four of them were the school outcasts, the nerds and the geeks and the loners. They were a club. They were tight.

He hid in the storage cupboard until break time was over, and then went to class. The afternoon passed slowly, and he kept thinking about the box he'd left on the kitchen table. He couldn't wait to get home and try to open it.

He didn't see his friends that afternoon, but as he walked home—taking the long way, in case Terry Nicks was hanging around for afters—he received a text from Lisa on his mobile phone. He felt his heart flutter, just like always, when he opened the text.

meet at mine 2nite? Mum's out at bingo. dad on niteshft. 8pm? bring the box.

He replied that he'd be there, and continued on his way.

When he arrived home his mum and Uncle Pete were upstairs, shouting. There were empty beer bottles on the kitchen draining board, and the curtains looked like they'd been closed all day.

The box was still on the kitchen table. They'd either not noticed it or had chosen to leave it alone. Sometimes they opened his post. If there was anything valuable in there—like a CD or a DVD he'd sent for—they often sold it down the pub.

Jack grabbed the box and took it upstairs. His mum's bedroom door slammed shut as he walked past, and he heard the familiar sound of a slap being administered. He went into his room and locked the door. He sat on his bed and looked at his monster posters, the books and magazines on his shelves and the DVDs in his collection. Occasionally stuff went missing. His mum and Uncle Pete denied all knowledge, but he knew that they stole his things. He wasn't bothered, not really. If he kicked up too much of a fuss, he'd get a slap, and he could do without the pain.

His friends had been right about the box. He tried to slide his fingers under the cardboard flaps at the top and peel them down, but they wouldn't move. It seemed impossible, but they were sealed, with no gaps. When he took out his penknife and tried to cut one side of the box, he had no success. There were no joins, either; the box was constructed out of a single sheet of material, folded carefully.

"This is weird," he said. Then he was distracted by the sound of his mum and Uncle Pete making the headboard bang against the wall. When his mum's moaning became too loud to bear, he put in his headphones and listened to some music. Loud music. The loudest he could find on his playlists.

He left the house at 7:45. Lisa lived a few streets away, and it wouldn't take him long to get there. He'd been lucky enough not to run into his mum and Uncle Pete as he made a sandwich in the kitchen, and then ate it watching TV in the front room. They must be too drunk to bother with coming downstairs. They did that sometimes, stayed on the second floor all day, only coming down at night to listen to music, shout some more at each other, and order a takeaway long after midnight.

Jack wondered if everyone's life was like this—or was it just him? What had he ever done to deserve this? He was a good boy, he stuck in at school, stayed out of trouble...but for some reason his life had turned to shit.

He missed his dad. He missed him so much that he knew if he started crying he would never, ever stop. So he never cried. He kept it all locked down inside, with a lid on. He was never going to let that particular monster out of that particular box.

The others were already there when he arrived at Lisa's place. She kissed him on the cheek as she let him in. He felt his cheeks flush.

"I'm glad you came," she said. She was wearing a pair of dark denim jeans and a T-shirt with a monkey's face on the front. Her feet were bare. She was wearing her hair down, and it hung across her shoulders in silken splendour.

"Me, too," he said, as he followed her upstairs to her room. He tried not to look at her bottom. But these days he found it hard not to look at Lisa in that way. She was a pretty girl. Whenever she smiled at him, he felt hot and anxious. He didn't know if Bill and Scott felt the same way; they'd never discussed it. It was a topic they steered clear of.

"Hi," said Bill without looking up as they entered the room.

Scott, sitting on the bed, raised a hand in greeting.

There were three cardboard boxes on the floor next to Bill. Jack walked over and added his own box to the group.

"Okay," he said. "What's happening?"

Bill stood and faced the room. "I have a theory."

"Here we go..." said Lisa. Scott giggled from the bed. Jack smiled.

"No, seriously. Listen. You've heard of Pandora's Box, right? Where all the evils in the world were held, until that silly bint opened it?"

"Oi," said Lisa. "Less of the sexism, please!"

Scott giggled again, and Jack realised that he was nervous.

"I think what we have here," said Bill, approaching the boxes, "is the same thing. But instead of one box, we have four."

"That's a bit of a stretch," said Jack. "I mean, what made you even think that?"

Bill shrugged. "I don't see you lot coming up with any ideas."

"I think they're from aliens," said Scott, shifting on the bed. "They're gifts..." He glanced up, at the ceiling. "Gifts from above. I saw a film once, where aliens sent down a big black slab to help humans evolve..."

"You boys don't half talk a lot of crap," said Lisa. She sat down facing the boxes. "Hey, look at this...they've changed."

Scott slid off the end of the bed. Bill flopped down heavily opposite Lisa. Jack walked over and crouched, staring at the boxes.

"You're right," said Bill.

The boxes had changed colour. Now, instead of the dull manila colour of normal cardboard boxes, they'd turned white, as white as bleached bone. And the flaps at the top of each box had opened, puckering out like strange petals.

"Whoa..." Bill leaned forward. "This is getting really weird now."

"Don't touch them," said Jack.

"Why not? Maybe we've been chosen... What if this really is some kind of gift, like Scott said?" Lisa was reaching out, reaching forward, towards the boxes. "From God, or something?"

"It just...doesn't feel right." Jack knew how lame he sounded, but something was nagging away at him. Why would anyone choose them to take responsibility for something like this? They were the losers, the mopers, the kids who nobody else wanted to be around because they didn't fit in. What could they possibly have to offer?

Before he could object further, Lisa had pushed aside the cardboard flaps on the nearest box and reached inside. She pulled out a mask. It was nothing special, just a dumb plastic novelty mask like the kind you could get from any joke shop. It was Frankenstein's Monster, all green-skinned and with crude stitching and black plastic bolts in its neck.

"What the hell?" Bill lifted out of his box a Dracula mask. White face. Black hair. Bloody fangs.

Scott's mask was a zombie. It had only one eye and its flesh was falling off, showing glimpses of the bone beneath.

"Your turn," said Lisa. Her eyes were wide. She looked...beautiful.

Jack reached inside the last box and pulled out the mask. His mask. It was a werewolf.

"What are we meant to do now?" Bill's voice was soft, almost a whisper.

"We put them on," said Lisa.

So they did.

When he got home later that night, Jack had no memory of what they'd done after putting on the masks. It was as if he'd suffered some kind of amnesia; his mind was a blank during the period between putting on the mask and leaving Lisa's house. He only recalled standing in the street and waving at his friends, bathed in sodium streetlight. The zombie, the Monster, and Dracula, all waving slowly, like weird characters from some kind of dream.

He sat in the kitchen with the lights turned out, staring through the eyeholes of the mask at the shapes of the cooker, the fridge, the sink. Each of the humdrum domestic objects looked different...but, no, it wasn't them that were different. It was him. It was Jack who had changed.

His mouth tasted coppery, like old pennies. His belly was full, as if he'd just eaten.

He reached up and caressed the plastic contours of the mask. Only it didn't feel like plastic anymore. He stroked the soft, warm pelt on his cheeks, probed at the fangs and incisors in his mouth, and prodded the thick, cold strings of saliva that hung from his lips.

He could quite easily take off the mask if he wanted to, but he didn't want to. He wanted to keep it on, forever.

He heard the stairs creak as someone came down. A light came on in the stairwell. He sniffed the air. It was Uncle Pete. Jack could smell the beer and the sex and the apathy coming off him in waves. He listened as the footsteps came down the stairs, across the floor, and stopped just inside the kitchen doorway.

"What the fuck are you doing sitting there in the dark?" His voice was slurred. He stumbled as he walked into the kitchen, slamming into the fridge with his shoulder. "Ouch," he said. "Bastard."

He opened the fridge, looked inside, raked around for a while, and then slammed the door shut. Then he walked over to the sink and filled a glass with cold water. His throat made a rapid *glug-glug* noise as he drank.

"Well?" He approached the table, pulled out a chair, and sat down opposite Jack. His bulk blocked out most of the workbench behind him.

"What the fuck?" He started laughing. "Why are you wearing that stupid mask? It ain't Halloween." He slammed both of his fists down on the wooden tabletop, clenched and unclenched his fingers. "Speak to me, boy."

Jack remained silent. He sat there with his hands in his lap, feeling the fingernails as they grew into long, sharp, lethal claws. It was an incredible sensation. He wished that it would never stop.

"Do you want this?" Uncle Pete raised his hand, opened it to display the sweaty palm. "I'll give it to you. You know I will. Free of charge." His large face shone, catching the light from the stairs. Sweat hung in droplets from his wrinkled forehead. His faded tattoos looked like dead veins seen through a thin layer of flesh. For the first time, Jack understood how weak this man really was.

"Don't even think about it." Jack's voice sounded to him like an animal growl. He wasn't sure if Uncle Pete had understood him, so he spoke again, slowly, just to clarify. "You touch me again, and you're dead."

Jack had never spoken so honestly in his life. His words cut through the untruths of the world and pierced the skin of a reality that was so much older, and so much purer, than the one inhabited by his mum and Uncle Pete. It was like a glimpse of a better place, one without the constraints imposed upon him by those who were meant to care but didn't, never had, never would.

Uncle Pete smiled. His eyes were empty. His teeth were yellow. He moved quickly for a man of his age, but nowhere near quickly enough. Compared to Jack, his flesh was slow and heavy; he was a monster from the new world, not the old.

Jack reached across the table with lightning speed. He swung his arm, the clawed hand taking a chunk out of Uncle Pete's throat and tearing away the bottom half of his face, exposing the bone of his chin. Uncle Pete slumped. His hand dropped back to the table, twitching. Blood pumped from the wound; it smelled of alcohol. Jack lapped it up anyway, or most of it. Something inside him began to grow.

Jack stood and walked away from the table, and then on impulse he dropped to all fours and padded up the stairs. It felt much better walking this way, more comfortable. Like it was how he was meant to move but he just hadn't realised.

He headed straight for his mum's room. She was sleeping. One of her arms was draped over the edge of the bed; her opposite leg was uncovered. Her skin was soft and white, like the material of the boxes once they had changed. Tiny hairs stood up to attention along her shin. He could see the veins under the surface of her skin, could hear the blood pumping through them. She smelled so much better than Uncle Pete, even if her body odour was stale.

Her feet were tiny. Her toes looked so damned tasty.

Jack stood on his rear legs and towered over the bed. He felt tall and strong, imbued with a power that he had never known he possessed. The mattress creaked as he pressed his legs against it. He bent down and kissed his mum on the side of the face, and as she smiled in her sleep he bit down deeply, wrenching away part of her jawbone along with the meat in his massive jaws.

He fed for a little while. Then he went back downstairs. He played with Uncle Pete's remains for a short time, tugging them around the kitchen, leaving red splashes and smears all over the linoleum floor. Soon he got bored of the game, so he went to the front door and opened it.

Outside, the moon shone down on the street like a theatre spotlight. The streetlights had gone out, but he didn't need them to see by—not with his new/old eyes, the eyes of the mask. Somehow they made it so he could see clearly in the dark, with the nocturnal vision of a nighttime predator.

All of his friends were out there waiting for him, and they were not alone. Hundreds of kids wearing masks were standing in the street, silently watching and waiting for him to join them. The doors of most of the houses stood open. A lot of the windows were broken.

Even Terry Nicks was there, wearing a mask that looked like a skull. His gang of bullies stood beside him, wearing their own masks. They nodded at Jack. He nodded back, reaching some kind of unspoken agreement. Old hatreds were now forgotten. There was other business at hand.

When Jack stood to his full height and howled at the moon, they all dropped to their knees, raising their heads and staring up at the cool, dark night sky. They clasped their hands together, as if they were praying, and rocked together, back and forth, back and forth, in silent mirth.

Some of them were wearing the masks of fictional creatures— similar to the ones worn by him and his friends. But others wore the masks of human monsters: serial killers, murderous despots and politicians, or the faces of everyday people who killed small children and buried their bodies on lonely moors. Where the masks had come from no longer mattered, just the simple fact that they were here, and they were being worn. Whatever was stirring inside him gave one final kick, and then it filled him, making him smile with his big, bad werewolf teeth.

Jack had never felt so alive, or so certain of his purpose.

Like a new king, he surveyed the eager crowd before him. These kids—these damaged vessels of innocence—now looked out from inside their bodies through the eyes of the monstrous, and what they saw out there in the world were the adults who no longer deserved to care for them; the real monsters, the ones that needed to be vanquished.

Because each child had received an identical box, and inside that box was not in fact every evil in the world, as Bill had theorised... No, inside every one of those boxes had been a mask, and something else besides. At the bottom of each box, waiting to be held aloft like a spear or a standard, there had been a little thing called hope.

Jack once more dropped to all fours and headed along the street, moving towards the rest of the streets that made up the town, and the ones that led to the wider world of rot and ruin beyond. He felt no fear, only hunger. He felt like he'd grown up and become something new.

Jack had left behind his childhood in the house that he was turning his back on, soaked in the blood of his irresponsible guardians.

He didn't miss his old life.

There was no turning back.

Now it was time to rouse his army and go to war.

WHAT'S OUT THERE?

JUST AFTER MIDNIGHT. THE INTERIOR lights reflect off the black window glass; too few stars punctuate the dark sky; clouds hide the moon. John walks across the kitchen, needing a drink of water. The tap makes a grinding sound as he turns it, and the water splutters as it starts to flow. He fills the glass, raises it to his lips, and drinks deeply of the cold liquid.

The lane outside is quiet and empty. He stares at the old, scarred stone wall opposite his window, the paved patio, the old potting shed that needs replacing because part of the roof blew off in a storm. Shadows stir, but that's all they are: formless shadows. He rinses the glass and puts it on the draining board.

As he is walking away from the sink, something bursts at speed through the cat flap. The noise is loud, fast, and full of panic. He stops moving, turns to watch the furred streak of his cat as she skids uncontrollably across the tiled floor.

"Whoa... What is it, Slinky?"

The cat slides into the far wall, coming to rest with her front legs apart, the claws unsheathed and splayed across the floor. The animal doesn't make a sound, just watches the now-silent cat flap.

John walks slowly and calmly over towards the animal. As he gets near, he bends over so that he is closer to the ground. "Come here, baby. It's okay." He puts out a hand, opens his fingers, and moves them, waggling them in the air.

The cat stares past him, her eyes big and scared-looking. The fur on the back of her neck stands on end; a cliché come to life.

The cat doesn't move as he picks her up, but her body tenses against him.

"Don't worry. There's nothing to be scared of. Was it a dog?" He rubs the cat's forehead with his thumb; she likes that. As he strokes her, he turns to face the door. The cat flap is getting old; the clear plastic hinged visor is grubby, so he can't see much of what lies beyond. But is that a small, misshapen shadow moving—or slouching—across his view on the other side of the door? He takes a few steps towards the door. The cat hisses. Her jaws begin to click in that way cats have when they're ready to attack. The specific sound—along with the jittery motion of the cat's jaws—has always unnerved him. He stops walking, but continues to stroke the cat's head.

He only puts down the cat when he thinks she's calmed down. Once her fur has returned to normal and she doesn't look so panicked. She sits down on the floor under the dining table and starts to clean her paws. John switches off the lights, climbs the stairs, and goes into the bathroom. He leaves the bathroom light off and opens the window, looking down into the lane below. It is quiet. There is nobody there. The lights on the main street don't do much to illuminate the private lane, but he's pretty sure there is nobody hiding behind the shed or sitting silently in the branches of the tree opposite the house next door.

He remembers one time when he heard strange noises outside late at night. This was back when Alice was ill. Tired, grumpy, he went downstairs and opened the door. On the patio, bravely standing its ground against four large house cats, was a fox. There was blood on its fur. The fox's eyes shone in the darkness, catching the light from his kitchen. The fox hissed; the cats slowly circled it. He noticed that one of the cats had a hunk of fur missing from its flank. Another of the cats was moving awkwardly, as if it had something wrong with one of its front paws.

He stood there fixated as in a single movement all four cats attacked the fox. By the time he'd come to his senses and run at them, chasing them off, the fox had been torn to pieces.

Picking up the bloodied pieces of fox, he'd put what remained into a black plastic bin bag. He tied the top of the bag and dumped it into his wheelie bin, deciding not to tell Alice about what had happened. In her state, she would overreact, seeing signs and omens where there were none. He hadn't slept much that night. He kept hearing those strange sounds in his head, sounds that he knew had been the screams of the fox.

He pulls his head back inside and closes the window. After cleaning his teeth, he walks across the landing to his bedroom. The curtains are already closed; the lamp is on. Slinky is lying on top of the bed, her eyelids flickering.

"Shoo, cat." He waves a hand near her face and she hops down off the bed, saunters over to the window, and pushes her way through the curtains to sit on her usual spot on the windowsill.

John is tired but he can't sleep. He checks his phone for missed calls or text messages, but finds evidence of neither. He resets his alarm to five minutes earlier than it has already been set for, switches off the lamp, and stares at the moving darkness. The fox screams inside his skull. He has not thought about that fox since it happened, but now he can't get it out of his head.

He turns over onto his side. The glowing digits on the bedside clock tell him it is 12:35AM.

John closes his eyes, sleeps, but does not dream.

The next morning John is too busy to even think about his cat's panicked entrance from the night before. He has to drive across town to inspect a property. There has been some kind of structural movement to a party wall. The owner is concerned that their house might fall down.

Driving through the morning traffic, he covers inches instead of miles. It takes him over an hour to do a fifteen-minute journey.

The house he is here to inspect is old; a Victorian detached property with a massive walled garden. An old woman answers the door. She is tall and thin, and still wears her white hair long, draped over her shoulders like a lace shawl.

"I'm John Trafford, from the building surveyors."

She smiles. "Please, do come in."

It doesn't take him long to realise that there is evidence of minor subsidence. The rear garden is on a slope; there is a history of mine workings in the area. But the cracks in the wall are cosmetic, so he doesn't have any bad news for the old lady.

"I'm so relieved," she says. "This house has been in my family for a long time."

She makes him tea, gives him biscuits, and tells him about her ancestry. He's heard it all before, in different forms on different visits to other people, but still he nods in all the right places, makes all the correct gestures. Despite the temptation, he doesn't check the time on his watch even once.

She waves at him from the doorstep as he pulls away. Right then, he suspects that she'd known all along what was wrong with the house wall. He found old repairs in the plaster. It is clearly an ongoing problem. Perhaps she simply wanted reassurance, or some company. He'd noticed there were photographs of her dead husband all over the house.

He finishes work early that afternoon. He doesn't have another appointment, and there is little paperwork to be done—and what there is can be filled in at home on his computer.

He feeds the cat, changes her water, and sits down to watch a football match he recorded a few days ago. He can't recall when. The days have blended into one; he no longer feels the passage of time. When Alice was still around, every day was different. Every smile was a variation on the last, like parts of an ongoing project. Each touch of her hand had thrilled him in a way that was subtly different from the time before. Unlike the old woman in the house with the moving walls, John does not have photographs of his dead spouse on display. He can't bear to see her face, not unless it's real. A photo isn't enough; it makes the pain more intense, reminds him that all he has is a series of carbon copies of the moments they shared.

The cat sidles up to him and begins to rub her face against his leg.

"Hey, Slinky..." He picks her up in his arms. She nuzzles his cheek, purring.

The cat had belonged to Alice. It was all she left him with.

Realising that it is getting late, he prepares a light dinner: pasta, with an olive oil and rocket salad. Simple fare; it was once Alice's go-to dish whenever she was in a hurry. The football match is over so he listens to music as he eats, barely even tasting the food. He watches the cat as she chases a plastic ball across the room, her small paws slashing.

Later that night, as he sits in his dressing gown reading *A Tale of Two Cities*, John feels his attention shifting from the page. He closes the book and puts it down, stands, and goes into the kitchen. He stares at the cat flap, but it doesn't move. Glancing out the kitchen window, he sees that the lane is empty. He kneels down beside the cat flap, shuffles closer, and waits, not quite sure what he is doing here.

Nothing stirs.

He pushes the flap with his finger. Chilly air wafts inside, but nothing else comes with it. He stands and opens the door, steps out into the darkness.

"Slinky..." Is that why he was compelled to come out here, because the cat isn't home? Jesus, what is he turning into, some sad bastard who worries more about a cat than he does about himself?

The night is still. There isn't even the sound of traffic on the road.

"Slinky... Are you out here? Come on, girl."

The air moves and brushes against his cheek. He twitches, and turns. There is something dangling from the low branches of the tree opposite the house next door. He crosses the lane, barely even feeling his bare feet against the uneven ground, and approaches the spot. As he gets closer, it begins to take shape. There is what looks like a bundle of rags hanging from a V formed by a meeting of two branches. Someone has slashed to ribbons a shirt or a coat and thrown it into the tree.

He moves closer. The rags become something familiar. Slinky's crushed little face stares at him from the mess of tattered meat. There is no blood, no bones, just her fur, with her head still attached. He wants to cry, but he can't. Knows that he should scream, but no sound will come. He is choked up with something—some emotion that he cannot understand.

Numb, he reaches out and disentangles her from the branches. She is floppy, empty; the cat she was is no longer there. He carries the dried carcass inside and sets it down on a dirty sheet, examining the remains. The cat has been flayed, but messily. The pelt is slit and slashed, but has for some reason been washed—or licked—clean.

What kind of predator is capable of this—or have some local kids decided to turn nasty? Turning towards the main road, he stares at the park railings, and pictures the housing estate on the other side of the park. This isn't a bad area, but sometimes he hears stories about gangs of youths straying from the estate to cause mischief. He thinks again of the fox, and of the four cats circling it. He imagines four people doing that to Slinky, his cat—Alice's cat, which she had loved so very, very much.

Then, gradually, the events of the previous night begin to come back to him. Slinky bolting scared into the house, her initial state of terror. The low, squat shape he'd glimpsed moving past the cat flap.

What kind of predator?

This wasn't done by children.

He wraps up Slinky's remains and puts them into a plastic bag, seals the top in a tight knot. He'll call the vet in the morning to have her properly disposed of. The vet might even be able to take a guess at what kind of animal has done this to a usually streetwise cat that is certainly no stranger to late-night alley fights.

"To be honest, I have no idea." The vet, Sally, straightens from her table and walks to the sink, where she washes her hands. She was an acquaintance of Alice's. That's how they ended up with the cat; it was a rescue animal and Sally had helped them adopt it. She drifted away when Alice died. Now, whenever he sees her, she acts as if they are strangers. "My gut reaction would be that somebody used a knife on her, but there are a few things that cause me to doubt that was the case."

John turns and walks to the window. It is raining; a light drizzle turns the world grey. The sun is trying to come out, but the dark, smeary clouds are doing their best to hold it back. The quality of the light is weird, imperfect, like an unfinished matte painting in a cheap film. He turns back to face the room. "What do you mean?"

"For a start, there are tooth marks. If a knife was used, whoever used it also bit into your cat." Her face is pale, serious. She is beautiful, but her features are hazy, as if he is unable to fix them completely in his field of vision.

"I'm still not sure what you mean."

"Neither am I, I'm afraid. Bottom line: whoever or whatever did this, it's weird. I have no frame of reference for what's been done to your cat. I'd suggest calling the police. That's all I can think of. I'm sorry... She was a gorgeous creature." A smile flickers across her lips, parting them to expose her tiny white teeth. John imagines them biting through flesh. "I know how much you cared for your animal. It's always...difficult when you have to say goodbye."

"Yes," says John, opening the door to leave. "Yes, it is."

After settling the bill with the receptionist, he heads straight home. Work can wait; they'll understand when he explains what has happened. He drives through the streets and looks carefully at the faces of the people he passes, wondering if one of them killed his cat. But who in their right mind would bite, skin, and then clean the remains of a simple house cat?

Back home, he thinks about preparing some food, but decides that he has no appetite. He does a little work, answers some emails, and then waits for the night to come.

Lately he does a lot of this: waiting, just waiting, for one thing or another. His life seems to have become a sequence of periods during which he is sitting or standing around, awaiting the arrival of something that never comes. Since Alice's death, nothing seems solid. It is all shifting, the edges blurring as he tries to stand his ground and prepare for the arrival of something that will change everything.

He thinks about the hospital waiting room and how much time

he'd spent there. The endless appointments with specialists and consultants, none of whom could tell him what was wrong with the woman he loved. Alice had been calm and patient, but he had felt himself crumble. Instead of being the one to help her fight whatever illness had decided to take her, he was the one who cried every night, needing her to hold him and tell him everything was going to be fine.

In Alice's time of need, he had failed her. He hadn't been there when she needed him most. He can try to justify it all he wants, but the truth is that he was weak, and she had slipped into the darkness without him being there to hold her hand as the light dimmed from her eyes.

That night he awakes long after midnight with the sense that a sound has disturbed him. It does not come again, but his skin bristles. Slipping out of bed, he puts on his clothes and pads downstairs. He leaves the lights off and sits down at the kitchen table. There are no sounds; the house is almost unbearably quiet.

"What's out there?" he whispers. "What is it?"

He glances at the cat flap and sees a small, blurred shape slipping past the grubby little plastic window. Gritting his teeth and clenching his fists, he stands and moves over to the door. He pauses there for a moment, taking deep breaths, and then opens the door to let in the still, northern night.

The lane is the same as always: dark, quiet, empty. But something is different, a detail that it takes him a few seconds to discern. On the patio opposite his house, there is a strange, yet familiar tableau: four scraggy cats standing in a circle around a fox. The fox has blood on its snout and its mouth is open. The cats are all injured; their fur is matted with blood; thin strips of flesh hang down from their sides, eyes and ears have been gouged by claws.

The strangest thing, though, is the absolute stillness. None of the animals are moving. They all stand there rigid, as if they have been stuffed, mounted and posed by an expert taxidermist with a taste for the macabre. Not a whisker twitches, not an eyelid droops, and not a claw flicks against the concrete paving stones.

John tries to move, but he isn't sure which way. In the end, he finds that he cannot move at all. Like the animals, he is frozen in place, waiting, waiting for something to develop. He senses that his presence is not important here; he is simply part of the background. Whatever is happening, he is peripheral, his role that of an extra. The main performance is yet to be played out.

The darkness in the alley seems to expand, and then to contract. There is the sound of something snapping—an elastic band, a tendon, perhaps even a small bone. Then, in that exact moment, the animals begin to move. The fox hisses. The cats walk in ever decreasing circles around their prey, their movements jerky and awkward—puppet-like. John looks on, unable to intervene. Clumsily, the cats pounce, taking down the fox, and all he sees is the splash of blood, the rending of flesh and fur. All he hears is the fox's familiar screams, as if they are an echo of that other night so long ago.

When he looks up from the carnage and turns to his right, she is standing there, at the bottom of the lane, with the empty road behind her. She raises a hand, steps forward into a patch of illumination formed by one of the streetlamps. Her face is as white as paper, but the features sketched there undoubtedly belong to Alice. She is wearing a long white dress, ripped down the sides, seams tattered, torn hem trailing in the dirt at her bare feet. He cannot help but see her as a battered reminder of his cowardice.

"No..." A scream builds in his sternum, rising to his throat, and then peters out to a weak exhaled breath.

But this feels like part of the same performance as the killing of the fox. There is a ritualistic quality, as if each of these events is a separate movement in a preordained routine.

She starts to walk up the lane towards him, dragging her filthy feet. Her hair is matted with filth, with patches torn out to reveal the bare scalp beneath. During her funeral, there was a closed casket. She didn't look good at the end. One of her eyes is shut; the other one bulges obscenely from its socket. Her lips are moving, her teeth working at something inside her mouth. One hand keeps waving; the other is rigid at her side, as if she is unable to move it.

John backs away, his feet going out from under him as his heels catch on the step behind him. He falls down onto his backside, scrabbling in the dirt. Alice keeps coming; she keeps moving; she bears down upon him like a lion upon a felled wildebeest.

John raises his arms, shakes his head, and cries out something that might have been a word or just a muted scream.

She smiles, and when she opens her mouth he can see what it is she has been chewing. No, not chewing. Not exactly. Because chewed food is meant to be swallowed, and this is moving the other way. Fingers, a small hand is trying to force its way up from inside her throat. Her neck bulges, swelling like a horrific pregnancy. Her mouth keeps opening, yawning beyond any natural limit. The sounds coming from her are like strangled sobs. Another hand squirms alongside the first one, and as he watches, a miniature and incomplete version of himself forces its way up and out between her distended jaws. Alice's head snaps in two due to the enormous pressure, and her legs buckle, sending her down to the ground. She lands on her knees and stays there, swaying, as the small being climbs out of her, naked and dripping in some kind of red-tinted fluid.

John sits up, wondering if he can still get away if he moves quickly enough. Then he wonders if he really wants to get away, or if he'd rather stay here, with her, the woman he still loves.

Finally, her body crumples, going down in a bloodless, boneless heap, leaving John with an insight. What is left on the ground reminds him of Slinky: an entirely unsuitable vessel. This time it has chosen more wisely.

The small, moist form does not attack. It moves slowly, sinuously, as if the muscles and bones are still forming, and climbs into his lap. John strokes its soft, yielding head, feels the blood as it pumps slowly and hotly though its veins. Tenderly he kisses the top of its skull. The inchoate entity raises its face and looks up at him, its fathomless eyes filled with love, with compassion and understanding beyond measure. He gazes at features both ancient and ageless: sunken cheeks, a toothless mouth, a nub of a nose with only rudimentary nostrils through which to draw in air.

John smiles and holds the soft warm body close, ignoring the tightening grip around his chest, the way it causes him to catch his breath. Whatever it is—whatever he was waiting for—he has finally found it.

Thin bones knit together to form a solid framework; loose skin tightens across a rapidly developing frame.

They hold each other tight. Tighter still.

IT'S ALREADY GONE

I'M NOT SURE WHY I decided to look for the camera that morning, or even why I thought to look for it at all. Call it a whim; call it a random act of nostalgia. I just don't know. I don't know much about anything anymore.

I found it quickly, in one of the cardboard boxes standing in a line in the hallway against the wall. Near the top of the box, underneath one of her neatly folded sweaters, the one with the cat faces stitched across the chest. The camera was an entry-level digital model, years out of date. Basic. I couldn't even remember where we'd bought it, or the last time we'd used it—if we'd even used it at all. We were never a big family for photographs. We rarely took them, and when we did, they seemed to get forgotten about quickly.

The camera didn't need charging. It showed all four bars on the little icon, indicating a full battery. In retrospect, that fact alone should have struck me as odd, but it didn't.

I checked the camera and the memory card and there were no photographs saved on there. We'd probably never used it at all after cracking open the box it had come in. Like a lot of things that we'd brought into our lives, it had been set aside and ignored.

Back then, I was drinking a lot. We both were. It used to mess with our thought processes. We did things without thinking and forgot about them immediately afterwards.

I photographed the kitchen first. Just a few snapshots. I took a picture of the sink with the little window above it—its yellow curtains turned dull against the grubby glass. Another of the wooden table where we all used to sit and eat breakfast together at weekends. Then a few more taken at random, not even thinking about subject or composition. There was no real intent behind my actions. I was bored. Restless. I needed something to do but didn't know what.

When I scrolled back through the photos I'd taken, viewing them on the little screen at the back of the camera, I saw them again, in various natural poses. Helen was standing at the sink, sleeves rolled up, looking out the window. Sunlight in her hair. Then they were all sitting at the low table, frozen in the act of eating a meal—Helen and both kids, wan little smiles on their faces. In the last picture, one of Helen's legs could be seen in the doorway, the rest of her body having passed through. Flat surfaces in the kitchen. The kids' wide eyes. Their small hands.

I went through the house, taking pictures. Every room. The bedrooms were the worst; those pictures hit me the hardest. Helen was lying asleep in our double bed, the covers pulled down to expose her naked shoulders. Eyes shut tight. Arms outside the covers, hands held in loose fists.

The kids were in the bunk beds, covers pulled right up to their pale throats. Faces lost in shadow.

After that, I decided that I needed a whisky. I didn't care how early it was, that the sun was not yet past the yard arm. I just needed a drink, so I got one. I could never find any pots and pans to use to cook dinner, but somehow I always managed to put my hand to a bottle or a can.

With the whisky bottle in one hand and the camera in the other, I walked outside into the pale morning sunshine and stood in the front garden. The street was quiet; the school run was yet to begin. The lawn was overgrown, and the planted borders had been taken over by weeds. The hedges along the front of the property needed trimming back.

I rattled off a few more shots, this time of the outside of the house, making sure the windows were in the frame. Red brick. Timber door and window frames in need of a coat of paint.

When I looked at these new photos, the kids were visible in the living room, watching TV. They were sitting together on the sofa, as they always had done, faces wide open and taking it all in—enjoying the show. Their eyes shone with borrowed images.

Helen and I were in the kitchen. We were dancing, or that was how it looked. I was holding her, and she was holding me. Her head was resting upon my shoulder and my arms were wrapped around her waist. I couldn't tell if it was a memory or a fantasy of how things might have been. I'm sure we must have danced in that kitchen at some point, but I couldn't remember when, or to what music. We looked a little younger in the photos, but not much. At a guess, I'd have said a couple of years.

I switched off the camera and went back inside, sat on the bottom stair and drank again from the bottle. The house sealed me off from the sound of the outside world, keeping me safe. There were things going on beneath the surface that I couldn't understand—but I'd spent my life feeling that way, aware that what I saw wasn't necessarily what was really happening. The skin of the world was thin and whatever writhed beneath it was fat and sluggish.

The alcohol went down as easy as ever. It was like drinking juice. Tasteless juice.

I put the now half-empty bottle aside and went upstairs for a shower. Once I was dressed, I looked okay, as if I was just about holding things together. My eyes were redder than they should be, and my skin was pale, but I thought I could pass for sober.

Grabbing my car keys, I left the house and backed the car out of the driveway. It was a short drive to my sister's place, and I couldn't think of a reason to cancel our lunch. I had nothing else to do. Nowhere else to go.

Half an hour later, I was parking on the narrow street outside her house. I shut off the engine and watched a man delivering a parcel several doors down the street. He looked happy. He kept smiling to himself as he walked. His inner life was laid bare; he was the king of his own world.

I got out of the car and walked up the path to my sister's door. I wasn't sure why I'd brought the camera, but it was in my hand. I knocked on the door and waited for her to open it.

"Hi, Pete." Kathy looked tired. She always looked tired. "Come on in."

I followed her through to the kitchen. The place was messy, but it was cleaner than the last time I'd visited.

"You want some coffee?"

I nodded, sat down at the table and set down the camera in front of me.

"How've you been?" She didn't look me in the eye when she spoke. Instead, she busied herself making the coffee and pushing dirty breakfast dishes into the sink.

"The same. Always the same."

I sensed the tension in her body.

"Are you still drinking?"

I couldn't be bothered to lie. "Yeah...a little. Not as much as before. Mostly."

She sat down in the chair opposite and looked at my hands. It seemed like ages before she looked at my face. "Is that true, or just what you think I want to hear?"

I shrugged. "I still miss them. The pain doesn't go away. The only thing that helps is if I have a little drink."

"That's always been your way, hasn't it? A little drink. But you never did understand the damage it causes to the people around you. In time, all those little drinks add up to one big drunk."

"Very profound," I said.

She was being cruel to be kind. It wasn't helping.

"It's been eighteen months, Pete. They aren't coming back. They've moved away—far away from you and your 'little drinks'—and they're making a new life for themselves. You're probably never going to see them again. The quicker you accept that, the better it'll be for you."

"I...I still miss them." I was stuck in a loop; my vocabulary wouldn't move on from that phrase. The words defined what was left of my life.

Kathy reached out her hand across the table and brushed her fingertips against the side of my wrist. Her fingernails were ragged where she'd bitten them down to the wick. I could barely feel the contact; it was like being kissed by a shadow or touched by a small waft of air.

"Where did you get the camera?"

"I found it in a box. We must've bought it ages ago."

"I've never known you to take photos. I didn't think it was your thing."

She kept her hand where it was, resting gently against the skin of my wrist.

"Can I show you something?"

She took her hand away. "Of course. You can show me anything you want."

I picked up the camera and switched it on, accessing all the photos I'd taken earlier. I handed it to Kathy. "Look at these. Tell me what you see."

She raised the camera and began scrolling through the images. "I see the rooms of your house, and then the outside. Just pictures of your place. What's this about?"

My throat was dry. "Are there any people in the pictures?"

She shook her head. "No, Pete. There aren't any people. Just empty rooms and boxes you'll never take to the charity shop. You screwed it all up—you know you did. They won't be coming back." She put down the camera and stood, moving away from the table towards the fridge. "Is tuna salad okay? I made it earlier."

I felt like crying, but no tears would come. They never did. They just backed up inside me, creating a reservoir of pain. I had no idea how much of it I could take before the barriers came down and it all flooded out into the world.

As we ate, we talked about everyday things like the weather, politics, the sorry state of the local park and playground. It seemed to me that we'd pulled back from the truth to start juggling little lies, as if that was all we could do to hold back the darkness. I loved my sister and she loved me, but sometimes love isn't nearly enough to fix what's been broken.

After lunch, I went outside and looked at Kathy's garden. Despite the messy house, she liked to plant flowers, and keep things outside looking pretty for the kids. They'd be home from school soon. I knew they'd like to see me, but I didn't feel as if I could act like a normal person, not today.

Kneeling to take a closer look at the flowers, I grasped for beauty but couldn't quite get there. I reached out and rubbed a rose petal between my forefinger and thumb, some part of me expecting the colour to come off like dust on my fingers, exposing the fraud. Nothing seemed right; everything was slightly off, not quite what it was supposed to be.

I blamed the alcohol. Sometimes it put a filter across the world, making things seem vague and artificial.

I turned around and took a few pictures of the house, snapping them off quickly, before I changed my mind. When I looked at the images, there were no people standing behind the windows or in the doorway. There was nobody there; they were long gone. There was just a house and a garden and the memories of the people who used to visit this place.

I went back inside and kissed my sister goodbye. She used to smell of cheap perfume and cigarettes, but now she smelled of nothing.

"Same time next week?"

I looked at her tired face, those worn-out eyes of indeterminate colour. The dyed blonde hair that would never regain its former lustre, the sagging cheeks, the downy hairs on her upper lip. Unlike the filtered experience out in the garden, this was too much reality to take in. It felt like I was being force-fed an unpalatable truth. And how did I look to her? Did I even resemble the man I had once been?

"Yeah," I said, and turned away. I wanted to say more, to at least tell her that she was an anchor to me, but I didn't know how.

I drove back home with the radio on but couldn't find a song to help shape the moment. It was all too bland, lacking in depth or substance.

When I reached my house, I sat in the car for a while, staring at the windscreen but not through it—not *beyond* it. I tried, but my vision wouldn't stretch that far. The steering wheel was cold in my hands.

After a while, I got out of the car. For some reason I still don't understand, I raised the camera and took a single photo of the upper part of my house—the eaves and the slates on the roof. I stared through the viewfinder for a long time, trying to pick out something that shouldn't be there, but it didn't appear.

When I looked at the photo on the screen, some other me was standing there on the edge of the roof, staring right into the lens. This image of me held a whisky bottle in its hand. The expression on its face was largely unreadable, but it seemed to me that it contained at least a small amount of rage.

From my vantage point on the ground, I had no idea what I—or some version of me—was doing up there, on the roof.

Lowering my arm and letting the camera drop onto the ground, I turned to look at the street. A few cars passed by, but not one of them stopped. None of the drivers or the passengers paid me any attention. I was simply a man hanging out on his front lawn with a ghost of himself standing on the roof behind him. My world barely even interacted with theirs; they only touched at the edges.

The house loomed over me, casting a shadow I couldn't see. The world stopped breathing and for an instant it held its breath, suspending me there in the moment. I felt poised at the edge of something. When I looked down, the earth beneath my feet seemed to tremble, then the image blurred and began to shift. I saw grey tiles start to form and felt the sensation of being perched up high, looking down...

I closed my eyes. When I opened them again, everything was the same as before. Nothing had changed. I was not standing on the roof; I was rooted to the cold, hard earth. The broken camera lay at my feet. Somehow the whisky bottle was back in my hand. I had no recollection of going inside to get it.

I had the feeling that I had missed something, but only by a fraction of a second. It had been so close, this thing; close enough to catch a glimpse of, but not to touch. And now it might be gone forever.

I didn't dare turn around in case there was nothing more to see. No garden, no house, no landscape that I knew. I waited. Waited.

And slowly, softly, the world began to breathe again.

THE NIGHT JUST GOT DARKER

"We talked on, unmindful of the gathering shadows..."

- Robert W. Chambers

"The King in Yellow"

Dedicated to

Joel Lane

(1963-2013)

FOR A LONG TIME, I have pondered the idea of what it really means to tell stories. After what happened, and certainly during the continuing aftermath, the very notion of storytelling has begun to take on a much more sinister tone. We're all part of a story—indeed, aren't we all the main character in the story of our own lives? But what if those stories aren't everything they're cracked up to be? What if all our stories are subject to the whim of a single overworked author? Writing and rewriting; working and reworking, just to hold back the darkness.

These thoughts plague me in the middle of the night, when I find it difficult to sleep. When the darkness seems thicker, denser than it should, and the house across the street seems somehow more than empty. Most nights I'll go to my study and stare at the window across the way—the place where it all began for me. There's never anyone sitting there, but I can remember so clearly a time when there was.

My thoughts are always dark at these moments, during those long nights.

Sometimes I can cast them off in the morning. Usually they stay with me, darkening even the brightest of days.

I hate going to bed early. If I do, I'm usually unable to sleep peacefully for longer than a few hours at a time. Even as a child, I'd fight my parents' calls for me to go up to my room, staying up past my bedtime to watch something on television.

Early nights rarely agree with me; I have always been a creature of the late hours.

At some point during the night in question—in the long, quiet hours before dawn—I was sitting up in bed and staring at the greyish square of the window blind. It looked like a screen in the moment before moving pictures are projected onto its surface: bright, expectant, full of promise.

Darkness pressed in around me, but I did not feel trapped; I felt poised at the edge of an experience. Somewhere outside, perhaps as close as a few streets away, a car exhaust backfired. A dog barked. A bottle smashed against brick or stone. I glanced over at my wife, Kath, but she was still sleeping. I leaned over, trying to hear if she was breathing, but I could not make out a sound. Resisting the urge to touch her, I watched the gentle rise and fall of her chest.

Minutes passed. Or was it just seconds? Kath moaned in her sleep, turned over with her back to me. The moment—whatever it was—had been broken.

I shut my eyes, opened them again, and lay back down on the bed. It was no use. I couldn't sleep, not now that I was fully awake. My mind was racing but the thoughts were unclear. I knew the feeling well and often dreaded its arrival.

Rising slowly, so as not to disturb Kath, I slipped out of bed, left the room, and walked slowly along the landing. I was wearing only my boxer shorts—I rarely slept in anything else—but the heating had come on during the night, so I wasn't cold. The study door was open. I walked in, shutting the door behind me, and sat down at my desk by the window. The desk lamp was still on—I must have forgotten to switch it off earlier—and there was a novel open in front of me: *Treasure Island*, an old favourite. I picked up the book and began to read.

Before long, I glanced up from the page and out of the window. The front garden was overgrown. The privet hedges needed a trim. Our lawn looked sad and tired in the unforgiving light of the streetlamps. I allowed my gaze to roam, taking in the quiet street, the darkened houses. But in one house a light blazed from an upper floor window. From where I was sitting, I could see right into the room.

The man was there again, in the house opposite ours. He'd been there every night that week. I could see him through the open curtains. A small man, with thinning dark hair, sitting at a desk located in a similar position to the one in which I was seated. The house was but a few hundred yards away across the narrow street, so I could make out exactly what the man was doing: he was typing at a computer keyboard. Small spectacles with thin frames reflected meagre light. The man seemed to be concentrating furiously; the look on his face was intense. Every now and then one of his hands would come up and rub at his brow, as if pushing back an imaginary fringe of hair.

I'd never seen him prior to this week. This was a quiet

neighbourhood, where most people tended to keep to themselves. We didn't chat with the neighbours; there was never any reason to call on them for a social visit or to complain. We lived like strangers, barely even aware of each other's existence.

I put down my book and watched the man. He was lost in his work. Even from that distance, I could see the immense concentration that gripped his entire body, making him sit rigid in his chair.

As I stared, the man glanced up, stopped typing, and smiled, as if he'd known all along that he was being watched. The smile, though, was far from a happy expression. It was filled with what I could only describe as grief, or perhaps longing. It certainly did nothing for his drawn, gaunt features. Later, when I had occasion to think of the moment again, I decided that what I had seen in his smile was in fact a note of despair.

Unaccountably guilty, as if I'd been caught watching a woman undress, I felt myself blushing. Heat seared my cheeks. I blinked. Not knowing what else to do, I raised a hand and waved. The man in the window opposite took off his glasses, wiped them on a handkerchief, and then replaced them. He rubbed at his forehead in what I already thought of as his trademark gesture. Then he waved back, but slowly: a tiny, timid gesture in the night.

When he returned his attention to whatever he was writing, I felt lost for a moment, as if the late hour was about to swallow me up. I reached out and switched off the lamp, sat in the darkness for a little while longer, watching the man as he continued to work. His brow was knitted with concentration. He had eyes for nothing but the screen in front of him. I wondered what he was working on, what kind of task required such a high level of concentration.

After several more minutes, I left the room and went back to bed.

Kath was up before me the following morning. She pulled on her clothes and applied her makeup in front of the dressing table mirror as I incrementally entered the waking world. I wasn't sure at which point I'd managed to fall asleep, but it felt like I'd only shut my eyes five minutes ago.

Kath didn't speak to me; she ignored the fact that I was there, watching her through bleary eyes. I stared at her as she pulled on her trousers, admiring her long, slim legs. I felt an erection twitch into life beneath the duvet but tried to ignore it. We hadn't made love for over a month; so long that I couldn't even pinpoint the last time we'd done so.

"See you tonight," she said as she rushed out of the room. I didn't hear her go down the stairs, but I did hear the front door slam on her way out of the house. A sense of loss passed over me, as if I should be mourning something, but it only lasted for a couple of seconds before leaving me empty.

After staying there as long as I could, I finally got out of bed. Took a dump. Washed. Brushed my teeth. Ate a tasteless breakfast of toast and cereal. I switched on the television as I ate. Reports of street crime, corrupt politicians; a baby had been raped by an ageing pop star as its stoned mother watched. The news was depressing me, but I couldn't summon the energy to switch it off, so I kept watching, stuffing bland cereal into my mouth.

The bus into town was packed, as always. The buildings outside the window transformed from residential homes to warehouses and offices. The grubby canal wound its way along the same route. I put in my earphones and tried to listen to some Leonard Cohen, but the man occupying the seat in front of me was a constant distraction. The pages of his huge broadsheet newspaper flapped like the wings of a bird of prey, constantly drawing my gaze. I got off the bus a stop before the one I needed, glad to be back out in the open air. For a moment, I thought about turning around and walking home, calling in sick when I got there, and spending the day reading, watching TV, or listening to music.

But I did none of that. I went to work, sat at my desk, and crunched data for eight hours, wishing that I had the nerve to pack it in and do something else.

That evening I was home before Kath. She sent me a text message saying that she was staying out for a drink with her workmates and they might go for a curry later. I'd not met any of them before. She hadn't even spoken to me of them. It occurred to me then that we led separate lives, neither of which intersected at any point. Even the space we shared in our home was filled with compartments, and we passed by each other all the time without really connecting in any substantial way.

I made myself a bowl of soup and only consumed half of it. The rest went down the sink. My stomach felt heavy, as if my insides were turning to lead. Depression was a fly butting against a window pane; it buzzed and twitched at the edges of my day.

I tried to watch a film but couldn't maintain any interest. None of my books seemed interesting. Even music failed me. Everything sounded false, a poor replica of real emotions.

The man was at his window again when I went upstairs. Sitting at my desk, I watched him at his work, more brazenly this time, not caring if he saw me. I sipped at a glass of whisky, barely reading the emails I was opening on my laptop screen. Most of them were junk anyway: penis enlargement plans, payday loans, messages from fictional Nigerian bankers with money to launder. In the end I just gave up and watched the man, my whole attention focused on his presence.

It took him about an hour, but the man finally looked up from his work. He took off his glasses, wiped his mouth with the back of his hand, and stood. Leaning forward, he peered across the street, looking right at me. Smiling shyly, he made a little twitching motion with his head, and then beckoned with one hand. He was inviting me over.

"Me?" I said out loud, feeling foolish as I tapped my chest with my fingertips. "You want me to come and see you?"

As if he could hear me, the man nodded.

I think it was partly because I had nothing else to do, and partly because Kath had pissed me off by staying out with her friends, effectively underlining how little time we now had for each other. Maybe the reason doesn't even matter, just the fact that I went over there.

It was cold outside. I'd left my coat indoors but didn't want to turn back and fetch it. I hurried across the road, walked along the path, and knocked on the man's door. When nobody answered, I knocked again. The door slowly opened.

"Hello." He was shorter than me by about two inches, wearing a black T shirt, black jeans, and, as far as I could tell, black trainers. He opened the door further, backing away to allow me inside. Behind him, the house was dim. "Hi," he said. "Please, come in." Light glinted off the lenses of his spectacles. His skin was pale, his eyes bright and alert, and there was a couple of days' worth of dark stubble on his cheeks.

"I'm sorry...I don't even know what I'm doing here. I didn't mean to disturb you."

"It's fine," he said. "I don't get much company. Would you care for a drink?"

Once I was inside, he slid behind me and shut the door, then moved in front of me again and began to walk deeper into the house. "This way. The living room."

I followed him, looking at the monochrome and sepia-tinted framed photos on the hallway walls: family shots taken against a backdrop of industrial landscapes; dark skies behind empty factories and tower blocks. Inside, the house was the same layout as mine. He was already pouring the drinks as I entered the main room. There was a plain beige carpet on the floor, woodchip paper on the walls, an electric fire that didn't look as if it had ever been used. The furniture was nondescript. More of those rather bleak photographs hung on the walls. There were different people in each one. For some reason I decided that none of the families in the shots were his. He'd gathered together these photos. They comprised a strange collection.

"I hope whisky's okay?" He held up a glass, rolling it between his fingers. The amber liquid held inside it glistened.

"Thanks." I took the glass. We sipped our drinks for a while, enjoying the silence.

"So," he said, breaking it with his low, quick voice. "I've seen you across there, looking through your window."

"Yes...I'm sorry. I hope you didn't think I was spying on you. It's just that, well, our windows look onto each other." I smiled but it didn't feel right, so I dropped the expression.

The man shook his head. "No, I didn't think that. Not at all. But you're probably curious about what I do up there every night." He raised his eyebrows.

"A little," I said.

"I'm a writer."

My heart sank. He was going to bore me to death about his work. "Oh. I thought you might be."

The man nodded again.

"Have you been published?" I didn't really want to know; I only asked out of politeness.

"Yes, I have, but mainly by the independent press, in limited-edition printed books. I'm what they call a 'cult writer'." He almost spat those last two words out, as if they tasted of shit. His smile was brief and faded.

"I see."

We drank again. My glass was almost empty.

"Refill?" He didn't wait for me to respond, just poured me another. It was nice whisky, though, so I didn't complain.

"Are you a novelist?"

"Sometimes." He walked across to the sofa and sat down, indicated that I should do the same. "But short stories are mostly what I write." He rubbed his forehead with a small pale hand. "That's the form I'm most interested in, you see. It's the best vehicle for what I have to say."

I sat down in the armchair opposite. "Short stories, eh?"

"Mostly."

It was only then that I noticed the scratches on his arms. They were light, faded, old scars rather than fresh wounds, but I could see them through the coarse hair on his forearms. I'm still not sure why, but the sight of them filled me with a sense of dread. It was subtle, but it was there.

"Would I have heard of you?"

"Probably not." He licked his lips. Took another sip of whisky. "I write under a lot of different names."

"Short stories..." I was running out of things to say. What the hell was I doing there, anyway? I wondered if Kath might be home yet, or perhaps on her way, in a taxi. She would be confused if I wasn't there when she arrived home.

"Listen," I said. "I have to go. My wife...she'll be wondering where I am."

The man didn't move. He just sat there, looking at me. He wasn't threatening; he actually seemed rather sad and fragile, yet beneath it all I could detect strength of character. "Would you like to know what my stories are about?"

"I'm sorry. I really do have to go...my wife, you see..." But I didn't stand. I couldn't. Something was holding me back. I had the feeling that he was about to tell me something of great importance, provide a revelation that would change my life forever.

"I write about tragedy. Loss. Grief. Pain. All the tragedy in the universe. I write about human suffering to try and keep it on the page and stop it from getting loose in the world." His voice was modulated, but I could tell from his eyes that he was getting excited. "If I ever stop writing, it'll be free to roam, and everything will come to an end. The days will get shorter; the nights will get darker and darker until that's all there is, one eternal night." His tone was matter-of-fact. He didn't sound at all like a maniac, despite the madness of his words.

"That's...well, that's nice." I stood and walked backwards towards the door. "Thanks for the drink."

He smiled. "I'm sorry. I didn't mean to rant like that. It's just...well, my work is very important to me. It's what keeps me going. I spend so much time up there on my own, writing, that it begins to seem like nothing else matters." He stood, setting down his glass on a cluttered little table by the chair.

I couldn't resist one final parting comment: "Okay, but what about all the tragedy that's out there? The murdered children, the abused babies, the wars, the famines, the human evil... You haven't done a very good job keeping that at bay."

He paused for a moment before speaking, not moving an inch. Then his words broke the spell. "If that level of tragedy is already out there in the world, just think of the stuff that I actually manage to hold back. Can you even imagine what that might be like? What it would do to us all?"

I couldn't; didn't want to. "I really *do* have to go."

"Come back any time. You can read them if you like. My stories. I don't mind. Once they're set down on the page, they can't hurt you." He drank his whisky and flashed his spectacles at me. "Once they're written, I have power over them."

"Goodbye," I said, and turned, headed quickly for the front door. Once I was back out on the street, I glanced back at the main window. I could see him sitting there, in the same place, smiling; but then, when I looked upstairs at the window that was opposite mine, I could see him up there, too, sitting at his computer and typing his stories.

The whole thing was starting to feel like some kind of wind-up. There was a mischievous element to the man that made me think he was stringing me along with his nonsense about writing to hold back more tragedy. It sounded like a story someone like him would write. Perhaps it was even some weird kind of research.

I crossed the street and let myself back into the house. I was getting cold. I made myself a coffee and sat quietly at the kitchen table, cradling the cup between my hands, like I'd seen people do in adverts.

Kath didn't get home until very late. About 3AM. By that time, I was in bed. I pretended to be asleep as she stumbled into the room, giggling softly. She fell over when she took off her shoes, then again when she took off her clothes. She slid into bed naked, and was snoring within minutes of her head hitting the pillow.

Once I was sure she was under, I got up and went to my study, leaving off the light. He was still there, across the way, sitting in his window and writing his stories. He wasn't wearing a shirt, just a white wifebeater vest over his slim torso. This time I watched him longer than ever before; I sat there in the dark and watched him all night.

Once an hour he'd stop what he was doing and scratch at his arms with his fingernails, as if digging in deep. He didn't seem to be in any pain when he did this, but nor did he seem to enjoy it. He just did it, over and over again. From where I was sitting, I was unable to see what kind of damage he was doing to his arms, but I remembered those scratches I'd seen earlier.

It seemed to me that there was some kind of correlation between what he was writing and the minor injuries he was causing himself. I didn't want to think too hard about what that might be, so I tried to ignore his violent actions, focusing only on the act of writing. His hands moved so gracefully when he typed.

I woke up at my desk without even realising I'd been asleep, feeling as if someone had just left the room. The sun was up, but it didn't seem to brighten the day. The man was no longer at his spot in the window. I looked around, at the books on my shelves, the filing cabinet, the old sporting trophies in the glass-fronted cabinet, and wondered if they were really mine. I didn't feel as if I owned anything in my life. It was all borrowed from someone else. This feeling had haunted me for years, but I'd never known how to deal with it.

I went into the bedroom and stared at the unmade bed. Kath's clothes from last night were scattered upon the floor like the evidence of a sex crime. One of her shoes was by the window; the other one was under the dressing table. I could tell from the sense of absence that she was long gone. I wasn't sure if I even cared.

The next three days I spent away from home, working out of the Birmingham office. There was a big project going on and they needed the additional manpower. We worked ten-hour shifts, went out for a few beers afterwards, and then slept for a few hours before doing it all again. I was so busy that I forgot about my potentially crazy neighbour.

On the last night I found myself outside a pub in an area I didn't know. Somehow I'd lost my workmates, or perhaps they'd deliberately dumped me. I was leaning against the wall with a lit cigarette in my hand and no idea of how I'd come to be there. I didn't even smoke, not anymore. I'd given up—on Kath's insistence—a couple of years before, when we were trying for a baby that never arrived.

"Got a light?"

I glanced to my right. A young woman dressed in a skin-tight black top, a short purple dress, and knee-high boots was smiling at me.

"Well?" Her Brummie accent was strong. She had blue highlights in her long straight hair. There was a silver stud in her nose and some kind of tribal tattoo on the side of her neck. Her eyes were ringed with smeared dark makeup, as if they were bruised, or she'd been crying.

"Sorry...here." I passed her my cigarette and she used it to light the one in her hand. She sucked deeply from the cigarette, closed her eyes for a moment, and then handed mine back. I took one more drag and then stubbed it out against the wall.

"You're not from round here. I can tell by the accent."

"No. I'm from up north. Been working here."

"Ah. Right. My name's Cindy." She blew out smoke and it formed an aura around her head, obscuring her pretty face. "Wanna buy me a drink?"

"I'm married."

"So am I. Wanna buy me a drink?"

She shifted her weight from one foot to the other. Her cigarette was smoked right down to the filter, but she took one final drag before flicking it away. She smiled. Her teeth were small and very white. Her lips were thin.

"Why not."

We went back into the pub, and that was when I realised I'd never been inside before. I must have stopped for a smoke as I was passing. Christ knows who gave me the cigarette. I checked my pockets, but there was no packet. At least I still had my wallet and my hotel room key, even though I had no idea where the hotel was. I couldn't even remember what it was called. I suspected my drink had been spiked. I hoped I wouldn't pass out in this strange area, with nobody to help me. I didn't want to die here, on these unforgiving streets. I had unfinished business with Kath.

The jukebox music was too loud, causing the speakers to crackle. The pub was busy but not too crowded. We managed to get a table in the corner. I went to the bar and bought us both a double Jack Daniels and Coke—she was drinking it, so I'd simply followed suit.

"So," I said when I got back to the table. "What do you do?"

"What do you mean?" She was slowly nodding her head to the music; some kind of punk dirge I didn't care for.

"Like, for a job. Do you work?"

"Ah," she said. "This and that." She took a swallow of her drink. "On Tuesday and Saturday nights I strip for old married men in joints like this one. I go to uni part time, studying psychology. I write a blog. I do shifts behind the bar in a shitty working men's club in Digbeth." She paused, smiled. "This and that."

We talked for a little while longer, but I failed to register what was being said by either of us. The music was too loud. I was too drunk. The next thing I knew we were kissing. She had her tongue in my mouth and I was sucking at it hungrily. Without speaking, she stood and took my hand, leading me outside. We walked along a narrow pathway behind the pub, then down a set of decaying concrete steps that led to a canal towpath. The black waters glistened like oil. The sky above was almost starless, stretching away into a bleak infinity. It was pitch dark but somehow I could see every detail: Cindy's white skin, the tail of her tribal tattoo, the tiny scars at one corner of her mouth.

She led me to a small concrete shelter and took me inside. It was like a bus stop, but without any windows. I sat down on the hard concrete bench and she straddled me, reaching down to unzip my trousers as she kissed my face, my neck. She smelled sickly sweet; her breath was saturated in bourbon and Coke. I'd never been so hard in my life. Cindy wasn't wearing any underwear. She reached down and guided me inside her and we sat there, my arse going cold on the seat, her arse in my lap. She rocked gently back and forth, and then began to move more violently, eventually slamming her backside against my cock and balls. I kept slipping out and then back in again. It hurt, but it was a good pain. I came in less than a minute, but she kept on going. She failed to achieve an orgasm, but for some reason it didn't seem to bother her.

Cindy stood and adjusted her clothing, pulling her skirt down over her shaved crotch. I pulled up my trousers, feeling cold and alone. She smiled, laughed.

"Not bad," she said.

I had no comment.

She walked to the edge of the canal, looked down at the water. She held her arms tight against her sides, had her knees pressed together. Then, as if in a dream, she stepped out onto the water but did not break the surface. As I watched, she walked out into the middle of the canal. Beneath her booted feet, the water seemed to have the flexible solidity of rubber. I could see it distorting slightly under her weight, but she did not fall through. She kept going until she reached the other side and stepped up onto the opposite bank. When she turned around, she was grinning. "I've never been able to do that before," she whispered, yet I could hear her as if she were shouting.

My head was aching as if I'd been punched in the temple. I felt sick. Trying to stand, I was aware of the earth shifting, tilting, and I threw up down the front of my shirt. Glancing up, I saw Cindy waving to me from the opposite bank. She seemed farther away now, as if the entire bank were moving, retreating from me. A small figure stood behind her. Recognition trembled through me. The figure reached up a hand and rubbed its forehead.

"Don't go," I said, but I had no idea why.

Cindy's face held an expression of sadness. Her small white hand continued to wave, and then she was swallowed up by darkness as she followed the figure away from the canal's edge and into the trees.

I fell to my knees. There were no stars in the sky because they were all in my eyes. I saw exploding novas; the universe shrank and expanded all at once, sucking me in and then throwing me out.

When I woke up on the bench in the shelter it was early morning. Frost had formed an albino skin over the landscape. I walked back along the canal, looking for the steps that would lead me back up to the pub from the night before, but I either missed them entirely or was moving in the opposite direction. Eventually I saw buildings up ahead and off to the right. I scaled the earthen bank, cut through some trees and bushes, and emerged at the side of a main road. It didn't take long to flag down a taxi, and I showed him the name of my hotel on the key fob.

"You're a long way from home, mate," he said, pulling out into the light morning traffic.

"I know," I whispered, shivering and wondering if last night had really happened or if it had all been a drunken erotic dream.

When I got back home, I found a note from Kath. It was propped up against the salt cellar on the dining table, written in her usual messy handwritten script. The note said that she'd left me, but she wasn't sure if it was for good or just a temporary measure. She was staying at a friend's place and would contact me in a few days, once she'd made up her mind.

It was late afternoon. The sun was shuffling down behind the distant tower blocks. I sat and watched the television news for a while, trying to distract myself. There never seemed to be any good news to report. It was all about death and destruction, job losses and factory closures. I thought about the man across the street and got up out of my chair, moving over to the window. I opened a couple of slats on the blinds and peered out. There were no lights on in his house.

Unable to settle, I left the room. At the bottom of the stairs, just as I was about to climb up to my study, I spotted something on the floor beside the front door. An A4-sized manila envelope. When I picked up the envelope, I noted that there was nothing written or printed on it.

Returning to the living room, I sat down and opened the envelope. Inside was a sheet of typing paper. The title at the top of the page read "Canal Dream."

I started to read.

They walked along a narrow pathway behind the pub, then down a set of decaying concrete steps that led to a canal towpath. The black waters glistened like oil. The sky above was almost starless, stretching away into a bleak infinity. It was pitch dark but somehow he could see every detail: Cindy's white skin, the tail of her tribal tattoo, the tiny scars at one corner of her mouth.

She led him to a small concrete shelter and took him inside. It was like a bus stop, but without any windows. He sat down on the hard concrete bench and she straddled him, reaching down to unzip his trousers as she kissed his face, his neck.

She smelled sickly sweet; her breath was saturated in bourbon and Coke. He'd never been so hard in his life. Cindy wasn't wearing any underwear. She reached down and guided him inside her and they sat there, his arse going cold on the seat, her arse in his lap. She rocked gently back and forth, and then began to move more violently, eventually slamming her backside against his cock and balls. He kept slipping out and then back in again. It hurt, but it was a good pain. He came in less than a minute, but she kept on going. She failed to achieve an orgasm, but for some reason it didn't seem to bother her.

Cindy stood and adjusted her clothing, pulling her skirt down over her shaved crotch. He pulled up his trousers, feeling cold and alone. She smiled, laughed.

"Not bad," she said.

He had no comment.

She walked to the edge of the canal, looked down at the water. She held her arms tight against her sides, had her knees pressed together. Then, as if in a dream, she stepped out onto the water but did not break the surface. As he watched, she walked out into the middle of the canal. Beneath her booted feet, the water seemed to have the solidity of rubber. He could see it distorting slightly under her weight, but she did not fall through. She kept going until she reached the other side and stepped up onto the opposite bank. When she turned around, she was grinning. "I've never been able to do that before," she whispered, yet he could hear her as if she were shouting.

His head was aching as if he'd been punched in the temple. He felt sick. Trying to stand, he was aware of the earth shifting, tilting, and he threw up down the front of his shirt. Glancing up, he saw Cindy waving to him from the opposite bank. She seemed farther away now, as if the entire bank were moving, retreating from him.

"Don't go," he said, but he had no idea why.

Cindy's face held an expression of sadness. "Come to me," she said.

He walked out into the middle of the canal, amazed at how it supported his weight. It still looked like water, but it was solid; a pathway to epiphany.

Cindy beckoned to him from the other side of the canal. "Come on. You can make it across."

He continued walking, his skin numb and his mind travelling ahead of him. Before long he stepped onto the opposite bank, slipping briefly as he hit the incline. She reached out a hand and he took it. Her other hand was behind her back. He slipped again. She leaned towards him, gripping him tighter and tighter. Her other hand appeared from behind her back. Something glinted in her fist, catching the moonlight. It flashed through the air towards him. Because of his position a little way down the bank, he was looking up, his throat exposed. The sharp edge of the knife blade cut him clean across the Adam's apple, neatly bisecting it. He choked on bloody words that devolved into croaks. Falling to his knees, he looked up into her eyes. She was smiling.

He fell face down on the hard-packed earth and bled out into the night.

Cindy retreated into darkness, licking the blood from her fingers. She was nothing, not even a dream, or the rumour of a dream. Before long, it was as if she had never even existed.

I crumpled the sheet of paper in my fist but hung onto it, not wanting to let it go. My memory latched on to the image of that small figure on the canal bank, standing behind the woman who'd called herself Cindy. What was he doing there? Had he rewritten my own tragedy in order to save me, or to prove to me that he'd been telling the truth all along? Or had I imagined the whole thing? Was I hallucinating even now? At the time, I'd thought my drink had been spiked, but now I was certain. The way I'd come to outside that pub, the way I had followed the woman without even questioning her motives, the strange vision of her walking across the canal water, the figure in the shadows behind her. None of it could have been real.

I went to the front door and opened it. There was now a light on across the road. The man's upstairs room was occupied. Shutting the door, I stepped outside and went across the street. I walked up to his door and rang the bell. Keeping my finger on the buzzer, I tried to remain calm.

The door opened. He was standing there on the threshold in the same black T shirt, black trousers and black trainers he'd been wearing the first time we spoke. He rubbed his forehead, pushing back the hair to show me part of his scalp.

I wasted no time. "Who are you?"

"Call me Erik. With a K, I always liked that name."

"No, not your name...*who* are you?"

"I'm nobody, just a writer. I'm someone who writes stories."

"How did you know...how do you know what happened? Were you there? Or did you put the images inside my head?"

"I don't know what you mean. Please, you seem agitated. Why don't you come in?"

I followed him inside. This time he started climbing the stairs. "Up here. In my writing room. It's the cosiest part of the house. I have all the other radiators switched off because I only ever spend time up here."

Watching Erik's narrow, black-clad back, I climbed the stairs behind him. The lights were off apart from the one in his writing room; I could see the glow spilling across the landing and down the first few steps.

"This way," he said, entering the lighted room.

The walls of the small room were decorated with yet more photos of industrial landscapes, some with people in the foreground and some without. Several of them featured what looked like corpses under sheets or wrapped up in body bags. I suspected they were crime scene photos.

"Look at this," said Erik, rummaging in a drawer on his writing desk—a compact piece of mass-produced flat-pack furniture that was pushed up against the wall under the single window. He pressed a newspaper into my hands. It was a local paper, printed in Birmingham. The front page headline was about a series of murders; over the past six months the bodies of several men had been found with their throats cut down by some canal behind an old pub.

I looked up from the printed page and into his face. Behind the glasses, his eyes sparkled. "Do you see?"

Shaking my head, I dropped the newspaper onto the floor. The pages spread apart like skeins of slashed, bloodless flesh. My feet shuffled on the cheap carpet as I backed away, coming up against the opposite wall. I pressed the palms of my hands against the woodchip wallpaper. In the room's harsh light, I could make out more of those scratches on Erik's bare arms. Some of them had scabbed over; he must have drawn blood.

"What's happening here? What are you doing?"

He shook his head. "I'm a writer. I told you that. I write. That's all I do. I write it all down in the hope that it won't happen, and sometimes—just sometimes—it works." He gestured at the shelves on the walls. They were filled with black box-files. "All this...all my work. It's my *life's* work." He looked desperate, forlorn; he was reaching out, trying to make a connection, but he lacked the emotional tools to do it properly.

How long had he been doing this, and why? Who had set him out on this thankless task, this endless project? I imagined him sitting here for years, typing, scratching at his arms, his legs, other parts of his body I was unable to see. Pouring all of his justified rage at the world into these writings, imagining that he was making some kind of difference by noting it all down, transcribing the terrors he thought would happen if he didn't get them down onto the page.

It was pathetic. *He* was pathetic. A sad, pathetic little man...or was he? Had my experience last night shown me nothing? Was I going to ignore what had happened to me, mark it down as the result of a spiked drink and a raging libido? If that newspaper report was correct, then the only conclusion here—logical or otherwise—was that Erik had saved my life. He'd written a new ending to my late-night encounter, cannibalising my potential tragedy for one of his tales so that I might survive.

He moved towards me, not quickly, just at normal speed. I'm not sure why I reacted the way I did, but my hand made a fist and shot out, connecting with the side of his head as he approached me. He went down onto one knee, raised a hand to the point of impact, and blinked at me through the shiny lenses of his specs.

"I'm...I'm sorry," I said.

"It's okay. This must be confusing for you. It took me decades to understand what it was all about, and I'm still not even sure. I can appreciate your anger."

His lack of aggression made me feel more aggrieved. I stormed out of the room, down the stairs, and marched across the road. As I shut my front door, locking out the night and whatever madness it held, I glanced up at Erik's writing room window. He was already sitting in his chair, typing, as if none of this had happened. Just as I knew he would be.

The following day I called Kath on the phone. To my surprise, she answered straight away.

"Hello." Her voice was detached. There was a coldness there I'd not experienced before.

"We need to talk."

She laughed bitterly. "Jesus, were you always so clichéd?"

"Probably. Now, when are we going to fucking talk?"

"That's more like it. At last there's some fire in your belly."

I didn't respond.

"I don't want to talk, not to you. The time for talking is long gone. I've made a decision, and it's that I never want to see you again. I don't even want to come around for my stuff. I'll send someone with a van. They can collect it for me."

I stared at the wall, wishing that I could kick it down but knowing I was too weak to even try. "What did I ever do?"

"It's what you didn't do. You didn't love me enough. You didn't give me a baby. You never, ever understood me. You didn't even try."

The line went dead. She was gone; gone forever. Somehow, I'd imagined it being less abrupt.

I spent the rest of the weekend in a daze, drinking vodka, looking through old photographs of what I'd thought were happier times but were just the calm before the emotional storm. She wasn't smiling in any of them. Oh, there was the occasional half-smile, or an expression that seemed more than halfway there, but nothing you could ever describe as natural.

I'd never made her happy. That truth, more than any other, was tough to face. Thinking about it then, I realised that she'd never given me happiness either, not really. All we'd ever done was pretend. Our entire relationship was based on an idea of what couples were meant to do, what they were supposed to feel, rather than anything we'd really felt for each other.

Whenever I tried to sleep, my head was filled with images of that Birmingham canal, the girl walking out across the water, the small figure on the other side. The girl, Cindy, became Kath; the figure in the shadows was me, then it was Erik, and finally it was someone I'd never seen before. The stories were becoming confused, their plotlines knotting together to form a sticking point. The only common feature was Erik. He was the author of something much larger than himself.

By Sunday night I was sick and tired of drinking. The living room floor was littered with empty takeaway boxes. My clothes smelled of kebab meat and chili sauce. My mouth tasted like it belonged to someone else, a person who liked to lick under the rim of toilet bowls.

I didn't know what to do, so I ordered another takeaway. By the time the pizza arrived, I'd lost my appetite, so I threw it in the bin and drank the large bottle of no-name cola that came with it. I went up to my study, thinking that I might log on to the internet and watch some porn. Then I looked across the street and saw Erik sitting in his writing room window.

Things had changed since I'd last seen him.

He was naked—at least from the waist up. He looked thinner than before, almost to the point of emaciation. His pale, skinny arms were furred from countless new scratches. At that distance, I couldn't make out if there was any blood. His glasses hung at an angle on his narrow face. Even from my study I could see that his cheeks were shredded; the skin hung in thin, bloodless strips, like pages partially pulled from the spine of a book. Despite all of this, and his obvious discomfort, he kept on typing.

I left the house and walked across the street. It felt like it might be the last time. I knocked on his door, but there was no answer. When I tried the door, it was locked. Walking around the side of the house, I spotted an open kitchen window. He was in trouble. I had to help if I could. Never mind what he'd done, or what I thought he'd done; this was a situation I couldn't ignore.

I grabbed a nearby wheelie bin, moved it under the window, and used it to climb up onto the windowsill. The window was small, but I managed to lean through and unlatch the larger window from the inside and use that to gain access.

Once inside the house, I headed straight up to his room. There was a candle burning on the floor. The single light bulb hanging from the ceiling above his head had shattered; there were diamonds of glass on the floor around his chair. The glass in the picture frames on his wall had been broken. Some of it was bloody, as if he'd gone around punching them all.

"Hello..." I still didn't know what I was going to do. "Erik...are you okay?"

I could see now that he was in fact completely naked, but his legs were bent into an odd shape, the joints buckled out of true. They looked broken. He sat there like a man in a trance, just typing. His short but elegant fingers were the only part of his body that had not been mutilated. Every other inch of him sported a wound of some sort: a scratch, a cut, a livid welt.

All the tragedy in the universe... His words from our first meeting echoed inside my head, and then in the room. He'd been trying to make a connection, to tell me something important, and I'd ignored him. I wondered how many other people had done the same, until finally it had all become too much for him and had led to this point in time.

Slowly, I approached him from behind, reaching out to grab his gashed shoulder. The torn skin beneath my fingers felt warm, spongy, but there was no blood. "Please...stop."

He kept on typing.

I spun his chair around through one-hundred-and-eighty degrees, so that he was facing me. His fingers were still moving, as if he were still typing at the keyboard. Behind him, the keys continued to make a harsh clicking sound, as if his fingers still worked them.

...Just think of the stuff that I manage to hold back. Can you even imagine what that might be like?

"Please..."

His face was a mess. At the corners of his mouth, the cheeks were sliced clean through, like a Chelsea smile; I could see his yellowed teeth through the slits. His glasses were broken, the lenses shattered. But it didn't matter, because his eyes had been pushed deep into their sockets—perhaps by him, or perhaps by someone else, I couldn't be certain. His nose was flattened, as if from a heavy blow. His hair had almost totally fallen out, and he had two cauliflower ears, like those of a retired pugilist.

Despite everything, his hands still moved at the ends of his floppy wrists, the fingers typing steadily away at ghost keys.

"I don't understand."

He didn't answer me. He couldn't hear. Wherever he was now, it was cold and dark and silent, and there were more stories to tell. There were no stars, no moon, no hours of daylight. It was all one long, dark night, and he was lost within its silken folds. My rejection had sent him scampering into a fictional realm, a place where all the landscapes were bleak and industrial, and everyone was a stranger. I wondered if Cindy, the killer he'd written out of my plot, was there waiting for him, knife in hand, thin lips parted and ready to taste his blood...

I grabbed him again by the shoulders, trying not to think about how much they felt like raw meat, and lightly shook him. His toothless mouth dropped open; inside, darkness twitched and crawled up from the back of his throat like a thick black worm.

I felt tears on my cheeks. "Tell me how it ends," I whispered, choking back sobs. "Tell me how the story ends."

Erik's fingers finally stopped typing. Behind him, at the window, another kind of darkness—this one greater, blacker, and hungry—swept in from a distant place, covering the cars, the street, the houses. And that was when the truth finally hit me; that his stories truly mattered, had always mattered. Perhaps they were the only ones that ever would.

In English myth there exists the notion of the "sin-eater." The term refers to a person who, through the means of ritual, took on the sins of a household. They would be passed bread and ale over the dying body of a person, and by consuming these things they absorbed the dying person's sins and cleansed them for their passage into the afterlife.

This is called apotropaic magic; a type of magic intended to turn away harm. In modern times, might that role have mutated into something else? In an age of rampant commercialism and psychotic consumerism—times when all art is deemed useless, lacking real value—might not an artist adopt the role of a sin-eater for the whole of society? And if we are to accept this theory, who is to say that the job might not be entrusted to just one person, an obscure writer of dark fiction?

It is now six months since the unexplained death of the man I knew as Erik. Things have become worse, or so it seems. The nights are darker than they used to be. The days are no longer bright. I try to tell myself that it's coincidental, and the world was heading this way all along. Sometimes I even pretend to believe it.

Last night, when I turned on the evening news, there was a report about the recent mass shootings in Birmingham, Manchester, Leeds, and Newcastle: fifty-seven dead, another twenty still in critical condition. This was followed by an item about the East London rape gangs. Things like this never used to happen, not of such magnitude. Tragedy has accelerated; we, as a society, are nearing a kind of critical mass. There's no empathy left, no human compassion. Scenes like those I saw on television are now a common occurrence.

After watching the news for as long as I could, I switched off the television and went to bed. The manila envelope I'd found on the hallway floor was on my bedside table. I picked it up, paused for a moment, and then opened it. I already knew what I would find inside.

This time there was no story typed on the single A4 page. Just five words in bold font; a simple statement:

This is how the story ends.

WOUND CULTURE

CARRIE WAS UNDRESSING TO TAKE a shower when she noticed the new bruise. It formed a faint bluish line down her right thigh, a little like a vein but less defined, fuzzy at the edges where its colour turned and blended back to flesh tones.

She sat down naked on the edge of the bathtub and examined the bruise. Pressing her fingertips against it, she felt no pain. She rubbed the bruise with her thumb, but it didn't blanch. It looked fresh. She tried to remember if she'd walked into a table or a door frame, but had no memory of doing anything like that over the past few days. She wasn't a particularly clumsy person. People often told her that she moved with a quiet grace, like a dancer. She'd always liked the comparison.

Shrugging, she got to her feet, turned on the shower, and gave the bruise little more thought. The hot water soothed her, washing away the clinging strands of last night's poor-quality sleep. Nightmares had plagued her, but she couldn't recall any specific details.

When she came out of the bathroom, Dan was standing on the landing, combing his hair in the mirror at the top of the stairs. His handsome face was solemn; his hard eyes held a thousand-yard stare.

"Morning," she said. And when he ignored her, she said it again, louder this time.

"Oh, sorry, I was miles away."

She smiled and walked past him to the stairs. Dan was always miles away, usually miles deep inside himself, in fact.

They'd been married for three years now and as time went by, she became increasingly aware of his inherent narcissism. He spent hours looking at himself in the mirror; his own face was the thing he most wanted to see, and he took every chance he could to do so.

What hurt her even more than this evident self-love was the fact that he'd begun to ignore her. Nothing major, but an accumulation of small things. Like the situation a moment ago on the landing, or perhaps pouring himself a drink of an evening without even asking her if she wanted one. Each of these episodes added up to a sum of neglect that was starting to make her think she'd made the wrong choice with her life—that she'd have been better off turning down his marriage proposal that summer's night on Crete, when they'd been coming to the end of what felt at the time like a perfect holiday. But didn't everyone's life hinge on such decisions?

She thought again of the bruise on her thigh. It wasn't the first one she'd noticed recently. In fact, she'd borne several such marks over the last month. Perhaps it was the physical manifestation of Dan's casual neglect: small physical marks representing a psychological pain. The idea appealed to her, but she knew it was a fantasy, another stupid idea she hadn't thought through properly.

He walked into the kitchen as she was loading bread into the toaster.

"Two slices for me," he said, assuming that she would make him some without being asked. She slid the slices into the machine and pushed the switch.

"Coffee?"

"Mm-hmm," he said, eyes on the wall-mounted television she'd never wanted but he'd insisted upon installing anyway. Until this year he'd always spoken to her in full sentences. About six months ago she'd noticed these grunts and half-words beginning to dominate their verbal exchanges.

"Is there anything interesting happening in the world today?" The toast popped up; the kettle clicked to signify the water had boiled. The toast wasn't quite done how he liked it, but she put it on a plate anyway, a small, pathetic act of rebellion.

"Another mass shooting in America, Syrian refugees smothered to death in the back of a van, another politician caught abusing children. The usual crap."

Carrie winced at a sudden sharp pain in her side, as if a thin blade had sliced her there. She closed her eyes for a couple of seconds, and then continued making breakfast. She stirred the instant coffee and buttered the toast, then set it all down on the table before him.

Dan swooped down on his breakfast hawk-like, without a single word of thanks. She didn't like the noises he made when he ate. Why had she only just realised this?

After Dan left for work, she loaded the dishwasher and then sat down in the conservatory with a second cup of coffee. She worked from home, editing textbooks for a medium-sized academic publishing house. It didn't pay much, but Dan's job brought in the big bucks. She was happy this way, answering to no one, managing her own workload, not having to bother with people hanging around her all day.

The sun was warm; the conservatory turned into a sweatbox during the late summer months. She got up and opened the French doors to let in some air. A gentle breeze wafted inside, kissing her face. Birdsong filled the air, as if someone had increased the volume on the soundtrack of her life. The garden was abundant with life. The smells of the season hit her: freshly mown grass, the sap from the neighbour's trees, the scent of old smoke from a recently extinguished garden fire.

The sound of her phone buzzing caught her attention and she turned away from the view, grabbing the handset and checking who had sent her a text. It was Dan:

Sorry, will be home late tonight. Forgot to tell you I have a late meeting.

Bullshit. She knew all about his "secret" affairs—every one of them. With shop girls and secretaries and pretty little nobodies from the office IT section. She knew about every single one of them, and by now she hardly even cared. At first she'd been hurt, shocked even, but as the world continued to turn and the sun kept rising and setting, she realised that none of it mattered. None of it at all.

She finished her coffee and washed out the cat's dishes, refilling them with food and water. She hadn't seen Duke since last night, but the skinny little tomcat would be around somewhere. He liked to roam. Sometimes he brought back a bird or a mouse. He was a hunter, but not a very good one; he never killed his prey, just left it there, wounded and twitching, until she stepped in to put the suffering animal out of its misery.

Work was a chore that morning. She kept getting distracted by the radio news reports. She couldn't switch it off, she needed the radio to work; it kept her tethered to the rest of the world as she plodded through page after page of dry academic text.

The Syrian refugees had died from heat exhaustion while travelling illegally across a border in the back of a freight truck. Their bodies had been found jammed inside storage containers.

The politician had raped and possibly killed at least three children. This had happened twenty-nine years ago.

The shooting in America had happened at a kindergarten. It was unsure exactly how many fatalities were involved.

"What a fucking world..." She talked to herself a lot. It made her feel less alone. "Why do we do this to each other?" She preferred her own company to that of anyone else.

At lunchtime she went to the bathroom prior to making a sandwich. It hurt when she urinated, but not enough to cause her any concern. As she washed her hands, she looked in the mirror above the sink. More grey hairs amid the brown, a few extra wrinkles around her green eyes, and a small, dark bruise on her left cheekbone.

She turned off the taps and leaned closer to the mirror, inspecting the bruise. It looked like a shadow, but when she moved her head it remained in the same place. Touching it lightly, she felt no pain. She lifted her skirt and took another look at the bruise on her thigh. It was slightly darker, longer than before; a defined line running from knee to pelvis.

Did bruises grow in shape and size like this? She was sure that wasn't meant to happen. If anything, weren't they supposed to get smaller as they healed?

The light bulb above the sink flickered. It always did that—there was a faulty connection—but this time it seemed sinister. This time it felt like a message, or a warning.

When Dan got home later that evening, he smelled of whisky and perfume. Carrie was reading in bed—a pulp novel about an unfeasibly clever serial killer—and as her husband undressed, she watched him silently over the top of the book. He folded his clothes neatly and set them down on the tub chair in the corner, as he always did. He didn't seem drunk, but he'd always hidden signs of intoxication well. When he climbed into bed beside her, he finally spoke: "Sorry I'm so late."

"I hope she was a good fuck." She had no idea where that had come from. She hadn't planned to say it but was glad she had. Now that the words were out there, she couldn't take them back.

"What?"

"Whoever it was tonight, I hope she was good."

"I have no idea what you're talking about. I was at a late meeting, and then we went for a few drinks afterwards. Networking, you know. New clients. It's what keeps you in nice clothes." He was trying to sound reasonable, but she could sense his anger bubbling beneath the surface.

"Fuck you, Dan. I know. I've *always* known." She didn't even put down her book; she just held it there, staring at the page, as if she were still reading the story as she spoke to him.

"Go to sleep. You're not making any sense. We'll talk in the morning." He turned his back on her and within minutes he was snoring. Or pretending to.

Carrie put down her book on the bedside table and got out of bed. She pulled on a thick, oversized Adidas hoodie and a pair of slippers and went downstairs, out into the garden. She hadn't smoked a cigarette in over a year, but she took one out of the sealed pack she kept hidden in a kitchen cupboard in case of an emergency. Hesitating only a moment, she lit the cigarette and took a deep drag. She coughed, took another drag; this one went down smoother, better, like a balm.

There was another bruise on the back of her right hand, just below the wrist, ironically in the shape of a heart. It looked a little like someone had grabbed her there and held on tight—too tight, making a mark with two of their fingers. She rubbed the area and wasn't surprised to learn that there was no pain. There never was. No pain, just bruises.

She sat there for a long time, smoking and watching the sky above the high wooden garden fence until it began to brighten in the east. Carrie knew she should go back to bed, but she didn't want to lie down next to him. She never wanted to do that again. Something had changed; a shift had occurred, a possible fracture somewhere deep inside her.

She was sitting there still when Dan got up to go to work. He moved around noisily in the kitchen, making coffee, preparing his things, and didn't say a word. Ignored her, but more blatantly this time than he had done in the past.

Carrie found that she didn't care. She searched her heart for some kind of emotional response, but there was nothing. She felt nothing but nothing but nothing. It was a relief, if she was honest. There had been an unidentifiable absence in her life for longer than she'd cared to admit and now she was facing it head-on, and it was nothing at all like she had imagined.

The bruise on her hand had spread already, like some kind of disease or a fungal growth. Her hand, her fingers—all bruised, as if she had slammed them in a door or hit them with a large hammer. She flexed the hand, the fingers, and felt nothing. It was a strange and slightly exhilarating experience.

Dan had left the house without saying goodbye. She stood and went inside, leaving the doors wide open so that she could enjoy the morning birdsong. She filled the cat's bowls and called for him, but as usual he didn't come. Sometimes he stayed away for days and then returned ravenous, wolfing down two or three bowls of feed. During those times she was never afraid that he'd been hurt or killed; he was just the kind of cat who went on little adventures.

Dan had left the television on. There was a news report about an earthquake in L.A., the never-ending drought in Africa, three hundred members of a suicide cult in Jakarta who'd swallowed lemonade laced with cyanide.

Carrie drifted through the house like a ghost. She glanced at herself in mirrors and saw someone she could no longer recognise. Bruises now covered parts of her face, her neck, her throat. They looked like intricate tribal tattoos or heavy lace. She didn't pause to linger over them, just kept pacing the rooms of her house and wondering what had changed so fundamentally to make her this way.

She took off her clothes. Naked, she spun in slow circles, enjoying the way that her body felt so different from before, as if it belonged to someone else and she had merely borrowed it for a little while. She didn't want to give it back.

"My name is...my name. I am Carrie. Or am I?" Even her voice sounded different: bruised, ragged, as if someone had attempted to strangle her and damaged her voice box. "My name is Nothing. I am not here. This is not a miracle." Nonsense-words, spoken aloud just to hear her voice: a song; a poem; a lament.

She put on a T-shirt and some old jeans, slipped into an old leather bomber jacket, and went outside. Nobody looked in her direction as she walked along the street; they didn't notice the bruises on her face. She went into the shop on the corner and bought a newspaper and a soft drink. "Good morning," she said to the man behind the counter. "My name is Carrie."

The old man looked at her with sadness in his eyes, as if she were mad, and smiled and nodded. "Hello. Thank you." He took her money and refused to meet her gaze.

She sat for a while in a nearby café and read the paper, absorbing the tales of horror and despair. The bruises responded by throbbing, but not painfully. It was how she imagined a man's erection might feel: a tight pressure, a pleasant ache. Drinking weak tea, she thought about all the strife and troubles across the world and wondered if she might be able to absorb it all, taking everything inside of her and then pushing it outward, in the form of bruising upon her skin.

This notion was not unlike the one she'd entertained about Dan's emotional abuse marking her body, but it felt closer to some kind of truth.

"A little piece of me," she whispered. "The little piece in you will die." It was a line from a song whose title she could not remember.

She stayed out all day, ignoring her phone when Dan tried to call. "Not now," she said to the ringing phone. "Not ever again." Eventually she threw the handset into a skip behind a Chinese takeaway. She felt liberated; he could not find her. These streets were hers to explore, to enjoy. It was all hers to see through new eyes.

As the sky darkened, she roamed deeper into the city, entering areas that she knew were dangerous. Rundown housing estates, decrepit business districts filled with boarded-up factories and warehouses. But she walked unmolested. It was as if she moved unseen through this place.

A scrawny dog followed her for a while and then ran away. Discarded running shoes hung like an afterthought from a telephone wire. Car engines roared in the distance. Brakes squealed. People moved here in packs; they stalked like hunters, yet barely spared her a glance as they passed her by.

They were not looking for her. She was looking for something, but wasn't sure what it might be. Perhaps she'd know when she found it. But there were no guarantees; nothing was certain in her new world.

The rules had all changed.

She found the man on a street corner. He was parked up in his car with the engine idling, watching and waiting. She knew what he wanted. His need was as visible to her as the new markings on her skin. It branded him like black paint, or a layer of tar.

She approached the car and signalled for him to wind down the window.

"Would you like some company?"

The man nodded. "That would be nice." He had a pale, bland face, saggy cheeks, and narrow eyes of a colour she could not discern.

"Can I get in the car?"

"Please do." He opened the passenger door and she walked around and climbed inside. "How much?" He didn't seem nervous. He had done this before.

"What do you usually pay?"

He laughed. "That's a new one on me, love. They usually demand the cash up front and know exactly how much to ask for."

"I'm...new to this game. Just learning the ropes."

He put his chubby hand on her thigh. "You certainly have an interesting look. All those tattoos. It's weird...but I like it. I like weird. You might say I'm a connoisseur."

"Drive around the corner. That alleyway. Where nobody can see."

"Don't you have a room near here? That's how it usually works. Isn't there a pimp looking after you?"

"Like I said, I'm new to this. Freelance."

That gained her another appreciative burst of laughter. "Oh, I like you. I think I'm going to enjoy this one." He let off the handbrake and drove the car into the mouth of the alley, stopping halfway along. Up ahead, there was a dead end. Bins and heaped packing material lined the walls on both sides. The smell of rotting food hung heavy in the air.

"It's been a long time since I did it seedy like this, in a back alley behind a kebab shop." He was rubbing her thigh, his broad fingers gripping her slightly too tightly. The bruises there began to sing. She could hear them, like a chorus of castrati: high, beautiful, the voices of weeping angels.

"Why do you do this?" She looked at his face. It was a nice face, she decided, but with a hardness beneath the loose skin.

"Because I like it. My wife bores me, my kids hate me, and I need something to fill the gaps in my life." He leaned in close, stinking of beer and desperation. She noticed now that his eyes were different colours: one blue, one brown. "I have so many gaps in my life, and every one of them needs filling." He licked her cheek, leaving behind thick strings of saliva. "Are you going to help me do that?"

"I'm not sure I'm the one you need after all," she said, backing down, suddenly unsure of the situation and the nature of the line she might be crossing. "I think this was a mistake. I don't know what's going to happen if we stay here."

He reached out and grabbed her breasts, kneading them with those large hands of his, rough, impatient, a little too eager. "You know exactly what's going to happen. We both do. It's what always happens. I fuck you, I pay you, and then I leave you behind. My gaps are filled for a little while."

She squirmed away from him, pressing her back against the car door. "I think I made a mistake. I don't know who I am. I expected something else...something better to happen. This is not the miracle I was looking for."

"You can't back out now, not when my blood is up. You have to do something with this. It's your fault I have it anyway." He grabbed her hand and pressed it against his erection. The crotch of his pants was warm to the touch. He was panting for breath. "*Jesus...*" He pushed her hand away. "What the fuck is that? A disease?"

The mood had changed. Ice settled between them. She looked down at her hand. The bruises had joined up, forming large dark patches that were pulsating, becoming engorged, like swellings. Her skin crawled eagerly across her bones, as if it wanted to be free of her, to remove itself from the muscle and sinew beneath. It felt like a costume, something that didn't quite fit.

"I...I don't know." She held up her hand, pulled up her sleeve. The bruises on her arm were glowing faintly in the oily darkness.

"Get out of the car." He was on the verge of panic but just about holding it together. "I don't want this anymore."

"But what about your gaps? The ones you need to fill? I can do that for you...I see it now. Everything's becoming clear. I can help you. I think I can heal you."

"No." It was the last word he ever said.

The bruises on her hands and arms flowered, erupting like blooms of beautiful decay, filling the space between them with something that had never before been unleashed upon the world. Her body enlarged, the battered flesh erupting in a geyser. The bruised mass enfolded his head and shoulders, smothering him, turning his flesh to pulp in a matter of seconds as he struggled briefly, a fly caught in a choking web. Carrie felt her skin pulling away from her body, inflating like an air cushion in mid-collision, and it made her feel happy that she could consume this man's woes. The despair that she contained within her, that had been building for years, had finally found its ultimate expression. She was an artist without a brush, a sculptor whose clay was human flesh, a goddess giving salvation from destruction.

She fed. She filled his gaps and then her own.

All she left behind in the car, in the alley, was a shell. Whatever damage had been inside him, his omissions, his empty spaces, she had mended and sealed over, then taken everything out of him.

It took her a long time to walk home. Catching sight of herself in shop windows, car wing mirrors, and the windows of all the safe little homes along the way, she saw a tattooed warrior, a painted deity who had been born out of necessity into a world of need. Battered and bruised, torn and broken and twisted into a new shape, she would take what she needed and wait for the next step in her journey to be revealed.

What else could she do?

If Dan wasn't home, she would wait for him there, ready to receive whatever he had to offer. There was no way back now; all roads led to a destination she could not yet see. Her husband was simply another step along the way, an obstacle to overcome, a gap to be filled. A bruise to heal.

The bruises on her body throbbed in anticipation.

She had no idea what was going to happen next, but whatever it might be, she welcomed it.

PUBLICATION HISTORY

My Boy Builds Coffins
Black Static #46 (TTA Press), ed. Andy Cox, 2015

Some Pictures in an Album
Chiral Mad (Backwards Press), ed. Michael Bailey, 2012

Kaiju
Fearful Symmetries (ChiZine Publications), ed. Ellen Datlow, 2014

It Only Hurts on the Way Out
Previously unpublished

Kill All Monsters
Shadows & Tall Trees #3 (Undertow Press), ed. Michael Kelly, 2012

What We Mean When We Talk About the Dead
Shadows & Tall Trees #3 (Undertow Press), ed. Michael Kelly, 2012

Unicorn Meat
SQ Mag #20 (online), ed. Gerry Huntman, 2015

Cinder Images
Darker Minds (Dark Minds Press), ed. Ross Warren & Anthony Watson, 2012

Hard Knocks
Previously unpublished

Necropolis Beach
Black Static #51 (TTA Press), ed. Andy Cox, 2016

Tethered Dogs
Previously unpublished

The Hanging Boy
Black Room Manuscripts Vol. 4, ed. JR Park & Tracy Fahey, 2018

Little Boxes
Twisted Histories (Snow Books), ed. Scott Harrison, 2013

What's Out There?
Uncertainties Vol. 2 (Swan River Press), ed. Brian Showers, 2016

It's Already Gone
Previously unpublished

The Night Just Got Darker
Knightwatch Press (chapbook), 2015

Wound Culture
Previously unpublished

ABOUT THE AUTHOR

Gary McMahon is the author of the novels *Rain Dogs, Hungry Hearts, Pretty Little Dead Things, Dead Bad Things,* the *Concrete Grove* trilogy, *The Bones of You* and *The End.* His short fiction is collected in several volumes, including *Dirty Prayers, How to Make Monsters, Tales of the Weak & the Wounded, Where You Live* and *At Home in the Shadows.* His award-nominated fiction has been reprinted in various "Year's Best" anthologies and he has been nominated several times, as both writer and editor, for the British Fantasy Award. He lives in Yorkshire with his wife and son, and when he isn't writing he practices Shotokan karate.